Chris –
Thanks for your
friendship. This
dedication

Nuts!

A Fable

by

Robert M. Lebovitz

This novel is a work of fiction. Names, characters, characterizations, places, and events are products of the author's imagination or fictionally used. Any resemblance of the work's creatures or characters to actual persons, living or dead, or of its locale to actual places, as they are or as they were, is entirely coincidental.

ISBN 978-1-7325045-4-7

Dedication

This novel is dedicated to the election of 2020:
What we know will contend is more revealing than
what we presume it may yield.

Also by Robert M. Lebovitz:

To Be, and Not To Be: The Rise of Misplaced Power and What It May Foreshadow
A three volume novel of an Internet usurped to deceive and manipulate (823 pp).

We Never Do Wednesday's: Apart Together - A Couple's Alzheimer's Journey
A novel of acceptance (255 pp).

Nuts!

PROLOGUE

The people of Oakville love their park. It provides shade, beauty, and a venue for notable events. It's a place to play catch and hide-and-seek, for tourists and celebrants to pose for pictures. It's pleasant for all because of sensible rules: Dogs must be on a leash unless in the designated fenced area and their leavings must be picked up promptly; nothing wheeled is to be on the grass except for strollers, wagons, or small children's tricycles; pedestrians have the right of way on any of the paths whether paved or rough; and only the upright steel grills may be used for cookouts. As for the rest – picnicking, smoking and adult beverages, ball and frisbee games, tag, listening to music – good common sense applies. Few restrictive signs are necessary, since Oakville is a rational community. There are occasional uniformed patrols but only as a reflection of reasonable attentiveness and a rotating perk for the officers, one that must be earned as well as shared. Tradition, sensible habits, and watching out for each other seem to suffice.

Oak Park is a place for adults to relax, for children to play, and for dogs to amuse themselves and their owners. It's a place to have an alfresco lunch, to read, to listen for birds and identify them, to watch squirrels cavort and offer them small treats, or simply to nap or stare at scattered clouds.

The very stately and very old oaks, from which is derived the park's name, have been here a long time. Their vibrant fall coloration attracts visitors and residents alike. The unadorned branches of winter present a different, starker beauty that artists explore as well. The green leaves of spring create dense canopies. Oakville's climate is temperate, but being in their shade is welcome in the glare of a bright sun. The occasional brief shower can be escaped by standing under them. True, when the afternoon is oppressive with the heat and humidity of late summer or the rain is heavy or wind blown, the oak trees' protection may be insufficient. But such occasions are rare.

With the arrival of autumn the cycle restarts. The oak leaves again form great expanses of color – red, orange, yellow – which soon fall, as do the oaks' acorns. The people who enjoy Oak Park derive little from those often abundant tree nuts, except for the occasional pleasure – more centered on the children than the adults – of chasing and pelting each other with them. But these acorns do provide tangible benefit. Aside from being food for the squirrels, they're the origin of the new growth of oaks in the forest that surrounds Oakville. Even native stands of hardy oak trees require renewal. There are diseases and blights. There are strong winds in the spring and heavy loads of damp snow in the winter that break branches and sometimes bring a trunk crashing down. The saplings mature and eventually replace those that are lost or damaged, or are no longer fit.

The acorns provide another benefit that, although slight, is notable. With the maturation of the acorns comes the heightened activity of the tree squirrels to collect them. Then more inclined to tolerate human proximity, they chatter and chase, to the delight of many, as they compete to prepare to store them away for the coming winter. Not everyone is pleased by this more evident activity of the furry rodents, it's fair to say. Some would prefer their remaining high up in the trees, to thus be distant and "where they belong." But there is no escaping the fact that it's among these oaks and those of the surrounding forest that they live. It's not that they suddenly have appeared as much as a matter of being more evident.

Upright on haunches, paws pulled in, and eyes steady and black, it's hard to deny a curious squirrel some tidbit from the remains of a sandwich or packaged snack. The children are almost compelled to do so. The parents don't mind. They are abettors. It's precisely for such small adventures that they have brought their young ones to Oak Park. The pleasure is unidirectional, however, it seems. Rarely will a squirrel thereafter pause to look past what they've captured to the donor. Even then, it's but a brief moment of imagined contact. Its quick dash to acquire any offering is the only way a human could deduce that it's appreciative. How different that is from the workmanlike endeavors of the squirrels when they gather, without consuming, the acorns that are destined for their hidden caches.

Squirrels are superficially the same but certainly can tell each other apart. Their mating, their occasional posturing and aggression of one toward the other provide evidence of that. People who visit the park often, those who might sit alone on a bench to toss treats, may have identifiable favorites to which they attach nicknames honoring a physical characteristic or an imagined behavioral inclination – much as they might do with friends or colleagues or family members. The squirrels are unaware. The humans know it's for them to make use of such appellations.

Oak Park and its ancient trees are important to the people of Oakville. So important, in fact, that few give them any thought. This is often the way with very important, basic things, things that have been in place a long time and relied upon. The twin realities that they were once absent or could be lost do not come to mind. There is no reason to dwell on either. And that is the danger.

CHAPTER ONE

Oakville is a very pleasant and prosperous city. It's a fine place to live or, if circumstances made it so, to be from. While old, there aren't many who can relate the details of its early history or the true origin of its name. The City Librarian, Mrs. Black, certainly could, because she had used odd hours to scour the archives. She knew quite specifically when and by whose hand the majestic oaks of Oak Park, the Founders Oaks, were planted. Some would claim they must have sprouted from acorns buried by squirrels, since this is the way most oaks originate. Their exceptional age and size were simply the result of the park's fertile soil and the nearby creek.

Mrs. Black knew this wasn't the case, that, in fact, these oaks provide a home for the squirrels but were not initiated by them. She endeavored to keep these thoughts alive via her Saturday afternoon readings and her visits to the local schools. She put to good use the opportunities to explain that its name actually came about after it was recognized how much the stand of large hardwood trees in its park had become a symbol, how much the original twenty or so acres – which quickly was expanded to nearly thirty – had come to mean to the people who had chosen to live, work, and raise their children there.

The forest surrounding urban Oakville is vibrant and dense. But nowhere does it offer oaks as well spaced, with as broad canopies and as majestic outspreading of limbs as in Oak Park. Many wedding albums include pictures taken under their shade in springtime or with them as a colorful backdrop in autumn. The major difference between photos of recent years and those far older is how much larger and grander the more stately examples have grown. An early 20th century oil painting – in one dark corner of City Hall – makes the same statement, only with less realistic detail, which, if the matter is considered carefully, is of no consequence.

A few of those ancient oaks are hugely tall. But that is not the major reason for admiring them. In fact, being tall is not a prime arboreal virtue since it puts much of their bulk far up into the distance. Having achieved a grand height merely testifies to a particular tree's longevity and the twin good fortunes of rich soil and reliable ground water. No, it's the thick trunks, the implied strength and resilience of these ancient trees that are most highly valued. In prose and poetry, as well as in logos and trademarks, a mature oak is often used to represent strength. For the people of Oakville, however, it's the concrete reality of their thick trunks (a few, the oldest, are so massive that two men holding hands can't encircle them), of their heavy branches (often bowing low to the ground), and of the half year of luxurious foliage (although, the complexity of their bare branches can be dramatic against a bright, winter sky) that are compelling.

The hardwood of the oak tree is notable for yielding, to clever hands, a tough and dramatically grained finish. The Founders Oaks, being of European white oak stock, are of particularly high quality. But local crafts people must draw upon the surrounding forest. Commercial flooring and furniture makers likewise must be content with logging Oakville's environs. The Founders Oaks remain unique in the special protections they have been given.

Century or more old oaks are no longer to be found outside of Oak Park. Parts of the surrounding forest have no oaks at all, despite the instinctual efforts of squirrels to bury acorns to sustain them through cold, harsh winters. Human thoughts of the future were often outweighed by perceived immediate need. The taking of large oaks for firewood seems to have abated, at least, with the onset of a more ecologically oriented generation. So one can be optimistic. Nevertheless, commercial interest still exists and can override foresight.

To the chagrin of residents but delight of artisans, a wind or snow storm can yield a thick limb or two, even an entire tree. Fortunately, this only infrequently occurs, the latter almost never. But when any such opportunity does arise, it's quickly taken advantage of. There have been hints, unverified suspicions, that less scrupulous souls have abetted such "natural" damage. Oakville's citizens must be vigilant.

* * * * *

There are always squirrels in the canopy of the Founders Oaks. They provide habitat for animals of all sorts – large and small, diurnal and nocturnal. Because of the frequent human activity, the oaks tend to draw the more diminutive and less aggressive creatures, those which complement rather than intrude upon an urban setting – birds, for example, and inquisitive squirrels. Fall, the current season, is an especially busy time for the latter, with the acorns having matured.

On a bright and pleasantly mild early October Sunday, a family has spread out a blanket on the grass not far from one of the largest oaks in the park.

"Are they fighting," Victoria wants to know.

"No, silly," Nathan, her older and more self-assured brother, tells her. "They're just chasing each other. For fun."

"But they're making a funny sound. It sounds like they're –" she starts to insist.

"I think they're trying to gather up acorns and one might've taken one from the other," their father attempts to explain.

*** *CHAPTER 1* ***

"Sit down, Vicky," her mother says, "and finish your sandwich."

Victoria stares up into the branches of the big oak as she does so.

"I'd be scared to go all the way up there," she says.

"You'd be scared to go anywhere," Nathan teases.

Their father looks up at the scampering pair of squirrels. A small smile creases his cheeks.

"They must have sharp claws to be able to go up and down the trunk so fast, to hold on to the bark that way," he says.

"Do they bite?" Victoria asks.

"Yes. And they're coming for your sandwich if you don't finish it," her mother cautions, not as facetiously as she had intended since one has arrived nearby to stare at them.

"Big, nasty bites, Vicky," Nathan says as he claws the air and makes gnashing sounds near her ear. "Here it comes!"

"Stop that, Nate," Norman commands, with a glance at the particularly bold squirrel on the grass nearby. "Don't keep teasing her," he further responds to the startled look on his daughter's face. A large, strong man, stocky but not fat, he isn't shy about relaxing whenever he has the opportunity. Factory work keeps him busy during the day. Chores around their comfortable home with acreage occupies much of his otherwise "free" time. He lies back next to Victoria and gives her a smile meant to be comforting. "They won't bother us," he promises. "They just want to gather up acorns and put them away for the winter. It's their food for when there's nothing else. See?"

Norman points lazily at the squirrel that has picked up an acorn and, after a few nibbles to remove its rough base, has bulged out his cheek with it.

"He's eating it! Are they good to eat?" Victoria wonders. "Can we eat acorns?"

"They look dry and hard, Dad," Nathan observes. "I bet you could crack them open like a walnut. I still wouldn't want to eat one, though."

"I'll try one," says Victoria, aiming a bold look at her brother.

"No, you won't, my little girl. You'll do no such thing," says Marianne. She's more comfortable leaning back against the trunk of a tree than lying flat like her husband, but she welcomes the respite as much as he. She brushes some crumbs from her slacks, which cover shapely legs still evocative for Norman even though encased at the moment. He turns his head and grins at her.

"Acorns are seeds, nuts actually, so I guess they could be eaten. But not by us. They're way too bitter," he explains. "You wouldn't like it, Vicky. You'd spit it right out. You'd get sick if you didn't."

"What's bitter?" the little girl asks.

"You don't know what bitter is?!" Nathan exclaims. "That's dumb."

*** *CHAPTER 1* ***

"Tell her what it is then, if you're so smart," Norman tells his son.

"Bitter ... is ... bitter is ... It's ugh. You won't like it."

"Not an answer, Nate," his father rubs his chin and states. "You made fun, so tell your sister what bitter tastes like."

Nathan is silent for a few moments, then pretends to lose interest and picks up a cookie, which he's allowed since he's already finished both halves of one of the tuna salad sandwiches on wheat toast, just as he likes it, that Marianne had made for their picnic.

"It's hard to describe a taste, isn't it, big man," Norman eventually says with a smile. He looks at his daughter with great fondness, his chiseled features softened by what he feels. "Remember a few weeks ago, when we were blowing on the fuzz ball of one of those dandelions in the yard?"

Victoria nods her head solemnly.

"What did you do then?"

She shrugs her shoulders like the sweet, shy, slender, soon to bud flower that she is. Projecting so much of her mother, Norman finds it hard to mask that she's his favorite.

"You bit off one of the leaves, didn't you?"

Victoria makes a face that signifies remembrance.

"That's what bitter is," Norman instructs her. "You wouldn't want to eat something that tasted like that, would you?"

Victoria vigorously shakes her head No.

"Then why do they?" she protests.

"The squirrels? Because it's their food," her father ventures. "They're used to it, I suppose. Maybe, to them, it even tastes good. Not everyone likes the same things."

"I don't like green beans!" Nathan exclaims.

"See? And we three love them," Marianne laughs. "Isn't that the way it always is? What some like, others won't."

"There you go," says Norman. "Everyone likes different things. And that's fine, as long as you don't make someone eat what they don't like just because you do and think they should."

"Then why do you make me eat green beans?" Nathan inquires, his strong chin, which is much like his father's, slightly elevated.

Norman had responded quickly, without thinking of the implications. His son's rebuttal is so apt that he and Marianne only look at each other. Luckily, there comes the crunchy diversion of a pair of black SUVs on the coarse gravel. The family watches the vehicles slow, then stop. From both sides of each, men in dark suits and long, colorful ties step out.

Except for one, they are of similar shape and configuration – well fed and very well dressed. They clump together, seemingly examining several large oaks by the side of the drive. One – older, leaner, and, by his own manner and the deference shown by the others, evidently their leader – points to a particularly large example. The others admire it, then walk about, speaking in low tones and pointing here and there. The singular rough-looking man, in casual dress and lacking a tie, takes out a small notebook. Looking up and around several times, he makes an entry. Another of the group waves his hand, palm up, at something, presumably other trees in the distance. The note taker nods and makes another entry. Finally, ending their perusal to stand in a short line that stretches away from the picnicking family, they stare upward. Because the nearest is the biggest, he occludes the others. To the recumbent father they appear as one person for a moment before the group separates, the visitors individuated again but similar, like peas out of a pod. They return to their vehicles and are gone.

"Do you know about these big oaks," Norman says, prompted by the visitors' evident interest. "Have they ever talked about them in school?... Nate?" he pointedly needs to prompt.

"No, not in class," Nathan replies. "Misses Black, the library lady, used to read to us about them before she left. She seemed to know a lot about Oakville. Teacher never talks about Oakville, just about far off places."

"Well, the story of these very old oaks is good to know, since we live here. Actually Misses Black was the one who told it to me, to our whole class when I was about your age."

"Is she that old?" Victoria asks more with wonderment than curiosity.

*** *CHAPTER 1* ***

It's wonderful to be so young, Norman thinks. Still prone, he turns his gaze from Nathan to Victoria and pats the ground next to him so that the two should sit closer.

"It's from a book called *A History of Founders Oaks*," he starts. "Misses Black would read out loud from it, then ask questions so we'd be sure to remember. The book told about how, a very long time ago, more than two hundred years ago, in fact, people came here from Europe. They wanted to plant oak trees so it'd be like the land they left. White oak trees. Right here in this park. That was way before anyone you know was here. Way before your Grandma and Grandpa were even born. They knew, when they decided to move here, that they'd be homesick at first. This country was new and a bit scary. They wanted to have something from home, the big white oaks that they were used to seeing. So they brought seedlings with them. They brought baby white oak trees, I mean, in boxes of dirt. They carried them in their wagons all the way from where they first got off the boat. That was way before cars. Way before roads, even, really. They weren't sure where would be the best place for them to settle and had to explore around for a bit. Once they saw how good it was here – it wasn't called Oakville yet – they knew they were going to stay. They unloaded their boxes of dirt and planted the oak tree shoots right in this spot."

Nathan has a puzzled look. "Weren't there trees here when they came?" he quite reasonably asks.

"Oh, there were trees, sure. There were even oak trees. But they thought the ones from their old home would be better than what they expected to find here. They were pretty sure their white oaks would be bigger and stronger. When they were settled enough to have a city, they called it Oakville. Then, later, someone decided to call these big trees the Founders Oaks and made sure they were protected. They're never to be cut down or anything."

"I once saw them cut down a tree here," Nathan says.

"Well, that was probably what they call pruning, Nate. Not cutting it down but taking off branches that maybe were broken. Sometimes trees are damaged or get sick, just like people, so they have to, have to ... They have tree doctors that keep them healthy. Anyway, these very old white oak trees," he lazily waves one hand, "no one can just cut one down because they don't like it, or want the wood or anything like that."

A burst of high pitched chatter above them causes the family to look up as one. Two squirrels are hopping nimbly from branch to branch, scolding each other it seems, their tails upright. Another squirrel, impassive and still, sits near the end of a swaying limb. It's relatively close to the family of four and gives the appearance of watching them. Its tail is never still. It twitches this way and that. Several acorns are dislodged by the scampering pair above it and fall from the inner reaches of the oak's canopy, one landing on the family's blanket. Victoria picks it up and holds it out, as if offering it to the squirrel that is staring down at them.

Squirrels have eyes on either side of their heads. That is usually the way with creatures that are hunted by larger animals and must be alert to such dangers. Not typically preying on animals smaller than themselves, squirrels do not need to look ahead to track them. This squirrel, however, the one with the ceaselessly twitching tail, is unusual in that its eyes appear quite large, almost as if they were behind a pair of magnifying spectacles. Perhaps this is due to the contrast of the dark areas that encircle them.

Suddenly, two squirrels – perhaps, but not with any certainty those that were in conflict earlier – explode down the trunk of the tree. After a circuit of its base, they scurry up another, where they continue their argument amongst its heavy limbs. The squirrel with the acorn in its cheek follows after the squabblers, going up the back side of the same tree trunk and out of sight.

Relaxing, unperturbed, their picnic lunch so far a great success, the family has watched with some amusement.

"Now they *are* fighting, I'll bet," Nathan says as he stares upward.

"About what?" Victoria asks, somewhat timidly. "What would they have to be fighting about?"

"That's what I wonder sometimes," replies Marianne. She looks to her husband and gives him a warm smile to further soften the gentle jibe.

"Over the acorns, probably," Norman offers back. "This is the time of year when they put them away for the winter. They're probably arguing over one."

"But there are tons and tons around," Nathan says, waving his arms. "Why do they have to fight over them?"

"I don't know. I don't speak squirrel," his father says with a grin. "Like Mother said, I sometimes want to ask you guys the same."

"And I you, Honey, when you come home from work a sourpuss," Marianne smiles. Like any married couple who love each other without substantial qualifications, they have their conflicts, which melt away after a family dinner or are resolved via frank talk when only they are awake.

"Well, you said they were too bitter to eat. So why fight over them?"

Nathan's question, again, is reasonable. His father turns to lean on his side, one hand supporting his head.

"Too bitter for us, Nate. But squirrels like them. And the way they store them for the winter makes them less bitter, I suppose. They often dig little holes and bury them. See up there, near the top?" He points lazily to a jumble of twigs high in the near oak tree, many feet above where the chattering pairs of squirrels are still facing off. "That's one of their nests. They live up there, where they're safe from cats and dogs, things like that. And where the baby squirrels'll be safe – kits, we call them. Sometimes they put the acorns up there or in holes in the tree trunks. But usually they bury them."

"I've never seen a baby squirrel," Victoria says. "Could we get one and have it as a pet?"

"How do they find them after?" Nathan asks virtually simultaneously

"No, I don't think so," Marianne replies to her daughter's question. "They're only babies for a short time, in the spring. They need to stay with their mothers until they get big and then I don't think they'd make good pets."

"But they need their food in the winter," Norman continues. "So they remember where they buried the acorns and go get them later, when they're hungry." The joint, terse summary of squirrel life is a simplification and not entirely accurate, but it serves the moment. "It's good for the forest, too. Some of the acorns that they've buried in the ground sprout, become little oak trees. It's what keeps the forest full of trees even if some fall down or are cut down. Even some of these big trees started that way, I imagine, a long time ago."

"You're teasing, Daddy," Victoria protests, looking up. "How could something so big come from a tiny acorn."

The way their father takes a breath suggests that he's about to elaborate, perhaps to use her and her brother's origins as examples. He's on the cusp of noting her current petite frame and explaining how, soon, perhaps too soon, she'll be very big. Not willing to address those issues quite yet – he enjoys her still being a child – he refrains.

*** CHAPTER 1 ***

"They say that when there's a lot of acorns on the ground, like now," he segues, "it's a sign that a very cold winter is coming,"

"With tons of snow?" Nathan asks.

"Yes, several feet of snow for a while, maybe. That makes food harder for them to find and the stored away acorns even more important."

"Snow days! Snow days! No school snow days!" Nathan chants. "Super."

His response is pro forma. The truth is that Nathan likes school. He likes learning about new things. His father finds this trait admirable, feels it'll serve him well when he enters the more competitive world of high school. It's a another thought he's filed away to reconsider later on, when what he'll want to tell him will have a better chance of being understood and retained.

Victoria tears off a bit of her sandwich. She steps a few feet off the family's blanket before holding it out to the squirrel that sits on its haunches an the unsteady end of a branch. Another is watching from the crook of the same oak. The former, twitching its tail and staring at them with big eyes, appears more inquisitive. But this is merely how she interprets their behavior. It's impossible to know how a squirrel feels or what it's thinking or if it even thinks at all. With paws curled back upon its chest, it doesn't approach. To encourage it to do so, Victoria throws the scrap of bread and peanut butter on the ground near the base of the tree.

"Mustn't litter, Vicky," her mother admonishes.

"They'll eat it up, I bet," her father shrugs. "Come over here, Vicky, and watch. If you're still, maybe it'll come down."

As soon as she retreats the squirrel does exactly as predicted. Taking up the white morsel in its tiny mouth, it plays with it, its tail jerking up and down, side to side, before turning and running off. The other squirrel, flat against the bark at the crook of the tree, continues to watch passively.

* * * * *

At a nearby bench, Brevan Shannon has been watching the family's outing with a flat expression. He has nothing of his own to compare with it. The dry skin of his barely shaved face, which would wrinkle much the same with smile or frown, today has been dominated by the latter, his far more frequent mien. Lounging with one leg over the other, his moderately disheveled attire seems perfectly suitable for an unemployed unemployable taking his ease in the sun. Only, he's neither.

"Rats with bushy tails," he spits out. He nods toward the picnic blanket and its denizens. "I've been telling Bales for years that they're pests." George Martino, sitting adjacent, knows the motion is meant to signify the squirrels, not the relaxed family, when Shannon adds, "We should get rid of them."

"Well, he listens and wants to be reelected," Martino replies. "So you'd have to get people to complain, give him a reason to get rid of 'em even if it makes no sense."

"You can always have it make sense, believe me. You just have to put it the right way, and often. Besides, Mayor Bales'll get reelected. There's no doubt about that. That's my job," Shannon tells his friend. He runs a hand over a mass of unruly hair and looks down at his wrinkled dress shirt. A large stain near its breast pocket catches his eye. "I need to be more careful with the barbeque sauce."

"A few years ago the AC on my car stopped working. I didn't worry about it till it got warm, but then I had to take it in. You know what they found?" Martino puts to Shannon.

"What?"

"Some shit squirrel had built a nest by the firewall and ate through the goddamn wiring," Martino states. "Ate off the insulation then bit through the damn wires. Can you believe that?" he asks rhetorically. "Thick insulation and copper, and the rat ate right through 'em."

"I believe it. It's what they do. They're gnawers. With those big front teeth, if they didn't wear them down they'd get so big the little buggers wouldn't be able to eat. They'll gnaw on sheathing and trim. Even on a power line in the attic until it kills them. Too bad that's too late for them to pass the word on," Shannon laughs. "'Don't do that dumb shit,' they could tell the others. Bahh. Probably too dumb to learn. Just run on instinct."

"Is that so?" Martino teases.

"Yes, really, George. It's so."

"Yeah, well, most of 'em you line up to vote for Bales behave the same," Martino scoffs. Getting no reaction, he motions toward the quartet finishing up their picnic. "They seem to enjoy watching the nasty vermin," he observes.

"Yeah. That's the trick. Be cute. It makes people want to have them around. But, basically, they're rats with furry faces and bushy tails," Shannon states, "instead of beady eyes and shit-covered ass-whips. We should just get rid of them. Or, at least, not let them near us. I had some get in my attic and eat through the security wires, just like with your car. I didn't know about it, same as you. When I happened to think it was a good time to test the security battery, the damn system wasn't working. Could've had a break-in or the whole house burn up because of some bastard squirrels. I couldn't believe I never heard them up there. A whole family had settled in, the exterminator told me after. They found the nest in a corner and got rid of them but never did find where they got in."

"Trap 'em?" Martino asks.

"I suppose you could do that. But his crew stunned them with some kind of spray then gathered them up in a net."

"Good idea. Then take 'em out into the woods."

"That's what I thought, when he showed them to me, but he said no. They're territorial. They'd just come back. He killed them, I suppose. The little ones without much hair must have just been born, he said, and the reason he caught them so easily. Either way was fine with me, as long as he got rid of the bastards. They carry disease. Full of bacteria and fleas. Viruses too, probably. Too bad you can't just keep them out in the first place." Shannon resumes staring at the family. "See? See that?" he grumbles. "That's what I mean. Offer them an inch and they'll take a mile."

Shannon is reacting to the fact that, upon the little girl rejoining her family, another squirrel has run up to snatch the remains of a cookie just off the edge of their blanket. It scampers away, past the two others that have approached to sit upright and, so it seems, stare acquisitively at the mother putting what remains of their picnic back in a basket.

*   *   *   *   *

"Do you want any of these?" Marianne offers to the two children. "Vicky? Nate?" she serially inquires as she points to a plate of peeled, raw carrots. With their refusal clear and definite, she begins gathering up the other plates and cups.

Victoria looks up into the branches of the oak tree but sees no activity. The two squirrels have arrived at its base to passively watch. There's no way to know if they are equally curious and only less able to express it. Their posture suggests they are deliberately attentive, but this is merely the impression lent by their fixation on something that looks edible. Victoria picks up then throws a small piece of carrot as far as she can, which is not very. One of the alert squirrels makes a dash for it. The other waggles rhythmically and hops from side to side, almost as if it's moving to some inner music. Encouraged, Vicky holds out a much larger yellowish-orange root, intending to tempt the dancing squirrel to come closer. To everyone's surprise, yet another squirrel runs up instead, chattering loudly, almost to her feet. Although not as big as the others, its sudden appearance and rapid approach startles Victoria. She squeals and drops the carrot, which the animal retrieves then runs back, clawing its way quickly up the rough trunk. Whether from fright or simply surprise, Victoria begins to cry. Her father glares into the leafy distance then gets up to comfort her.

"Did it scratch your leg, Vicky? Let me see.... No, you're fine."

"I thought it was going to jump on me and bite me." Her face crinkles.

"It's all right. We wouldn't let anything happen. Would we, Daddy," Marianne says to soothe her daughter's reasonable sense of fright.

"Certainly not," he affirms.

"Next time I'll bring my BB gun," Nathan says protectively.

"No, young man. No, you won't," his mother tells him.

*** *CHAPTER 1* ***

The lad stands at the edge of the blanket and glowers out at the trees, trying to take on the firm persona of his father.

"Just let them try that again," he says and kicks out his foot.

*   *   *   *   *

"See? I told you. That's exactly what I mean," Shannon says to his friend, raising his arm to point at the four who are preparing to leave the park. "The damn pests were going to bite the little kid. She should never have offered them food."

"I don't know which is worse, Brev. Those flea bags or the people who encourage 'em. They should put up 'Do not feed the squirrels!' signs and stop encouraging the filthy things."

"Well," Shannon responds after a moment's consideration, "their instinct is to get what they don't have. Get easy pickings when and where they can. The squirrels, I mean. The kids think they're so cute – even the parents, some of them. Before the next council meeting I think I'll get with Bales. See if he won't push a resolution to get the park cleaned up. Put more restrictions on."

"I've seen people bring peanuts and throw them around for the squirrels," Martino says. "I can understand them chasing after peanuts. But I tried one of those acorns once. Ugh. Tasted like shit. Even if boiled, like the recipe suggested."

"You have an acorn recipe, George? Really?" Brevan says laughing. "That's ... Anyway, a peanut isn't a nut, you know. It's a legume," Shannon further informs him.

"Is an acorn?"

"Is an acorn a nut? Yes, because it comes off a tree."

"Then why does it taste like shit and peanuts taste good?" Martino wants to know.

Brevan has no answer to offer

"I remember reading," Martino adds thoughtfully, "that sparrows were once a big problem for the Chinks. In the countryside they were eating up the crops. In the cities they caused disease, they thought, and made messes for sure. So the Commies decided to kill 'em off. They made it a duty to bring in dead sparrows. An '... or else ...' sort of thing, you know, like they do. Anyway, everybody and his brother went around killing the birds. They used everything they could think of – poison, traps, guns, even rakes and sticks. They'd bang pots and pans to scare 'em away and keep 'em from settling. Exhausted 'em to death, I suppose. That's what we should do."

"Put a bounty on squirrels? Have everybody try to scare them off? Or shoot at them? It'll never happen, George. As much as I'd like to see it, it'll never happen. Not here. Not without a damn good reason." With that, Brevan Shannon goes quiet and looks off into space.

CHAPTER TWO

Safe in the trees, two squirrels look on with interest.

"Did you see that?" asks Caesar, the graying, middle-aged leader of the local troop. "The little one was nice enough to offer something, and Mel ran up and scared her."

"That's pure Mel, all right," offers Sandy. "Trying to make up for being small by being aggressive."

Sandy holds himself upright in the crook of the oak by gripping with sharp claws. The darkish line that separates his eyes makes him appear introspective, which he actually is. He angles one eye up toward the branch where Caesar sits. He's mature but not as old as Caesar, who's grown more inclined to imagine, and his incisors aren't nearly so prominent. Having less history than Caesar and none of his responsibilities, Sandy has more freedom for productive thought.

"He could've just taken it, like Twitch did. He ran down, snatched the treat the little one threw at him, then ran back up," he observes. "The child was pleased and so was he. That was the end of it. Take what's given then leave without being aggressive." Sandy looks to Caesar for some sign that he agrees. "Or, I hate to say, be cute like Beater over there, and just watch. Let them watch you. Be playful and everything's fine. Just don't do like that damn Mel."

Twitch is not far from the two critics, still chewing and his tail jerking constantly. His more forward facing but not very acute eyes – some tease that his father was a prairie dog, so as to account for his perpetual state of nervous agitation – lend him a studious appearance. This, however, is far from the fact. While he might look like he's peering thoughtfully, perhaps through a pair of assistive lenses, he's merely struggling to see what others find apparent.

"Mel's lucky, you know," Caesar muses aloud. "That could've been the end of him."

Sandy doesn't care for Mel's attitude, never has, but doesn't understand why it much matters for his longevity.

"How's that?" he asks.

"Those old men on the bench. Over there, see?" Caesar cants his head in their general direction. "I've seen their kind walking the woods with shotguns. Killed a lot of us. Just for fun, too, it seemed. There's nothing says they can't, when they're deep enough into forest. Not every human thinks we're fun to watch. Actually, some like us for target practice, a way to show off their skill with a gun and at the same time release a little aggression."

"Like Mel there did?"

Caesar studies Sandy a long time before responding.

"Yes, good point. We're not innocent. And today those two humans on the bench seemed annoyed."

Sandy scrambles up into the foliage and looks down suspiciously.

"Is that what they're going to do, you think? Get out guns? What did they say?"

"How should I know?" Caesar tells Sandy. "I can guess, though, by the expressions on their faces and how they waved their hands about, that they were annoyed. You don't have to understand their talk to pick that up. I'm glad we're here and not off somewhere deep in the woods. We're supposed to be safe here, but we'd better not count on it. Mel certainly shouldn't have."

Beater, having scampered back up the rough trunk and now perched at the end of a thin canopy branch, resumes his characteristic rhythmic chattering. This, in time with his shifting posture, is not typical of squirrels and makes his given name highly appropriate. Caesar tilts his head upward to get a better look at him.

"He didn't get a thing," he notes. "The other one – Petey, I think it was – beat him to it. Beat Beater to it," he chuckles.

*** *CHAPTER 2* ***

"Why does his hair stick up like that?" Sandy asks Caesar, not really expecting an answer. "He always looks like he's just bit into some wiring in house. Do you understand what he's going on about?" is his follow up, for which he really does.

"Are you kidding?" Caesar sighs after a moment's pause. "Understand Beater? I've given up on that. He's as obscure as the humans. I can get some of it. But, the way he doubles his words and strings them together?" He shakes his head. "No. He doesn't make sense to me most of the time." Working his lower jaw as if chewing, he pulls his forepaws close in. "Fun to watch, though."

"Beryl made it back with two acorns this time," Sandy observes, peering back and up to see where he might have gone. "He's going to choke himself one of these days, always trying to take on more than he can handle."

Caesar bobs his head in agreement.

"You're right," he says. "He'll come to a bad end – get run over by a bike or a car probably. You can be sure of that."

Caesar and Sandy watch Beater hopping from side to side, striking his curious poses and holding one for a few seconds before jerking himself into another.

"It's silly, but I suppose Beater's doing what we all need to do," Caesar sighs. "Show them, the humans, how cute we can be." He angles himself toward Sandy. "I'm getting too old for that, I'm afraid. But I have to admit I've grown tired of acorn. If we were cuter and more pleasant, maybe they'd bring more nuts and tasties for us, not just throw leftover scraps." He looks down, watching Twitch enjoy his and waiting for some reply from his companion. None forthcoming he goes on. "Remember the actual peanuts that man threw out, just after the snow melted and the first humans were having their picnics? Now there's a treat. Easy to open and a lot tastier than ..." He works his lower jaw back and forth sideways several times without finishing. "Well, anyway."

With this, the curmudgeonly elder lets the matter lie. He knows he's repeating himself, merely expressing the frustrations that come with seniority. Pushing aside any deeper implications, he focuses his attention on Beater once more. How can that barely mature exhibitionist stay in place on the swaying branch? he silently wonders. He'd be too engrossed with his own antics to grab at anything if he fell off.

"Wouldn't mind if he did," Caesar says aloud.

"If who did what?" asks Sandy. Not privy to Caesar's ruminations, he's been mulling over the very reasonable peanut possibility and is mystified by the sudden change in direction.

"If Beater fell off on his ass," Caesar clarifies.

"He's done that more than once and isn't the worse for it," Sandy observes. He, also, looks down and around. "It's safe enough," he adds. "Doesn't look like there are any dogs around today."

*** *CHAPTER 2* ***

"Where did he go with it?" Caesar asks. "Mel with his stolen treat, I mean."

"The carrot? Why do you shift from one topic to another like that? Your mind jumps around like Beater's butt. It's hard to follow you sometimes," Sandy tells him. He lifts himself upright and stares into the greenery. "Anyway, Mel's in there somewhere," he then answers back with a quick turn of his head as he drops to all fours, "in the thick of the leaves. I think I saw him follow Mae up. Had it dangling out from his mouth.... What the hell does he want with a carrot, anyway? It'll just rot if he doesn't eat it."

They cannot see, because they're on the other side of the tree, but Mel is indeed with Mae. He's alert and the carrot is now tightly gripped by his forepaws, just in case one of the other squirrels should try to steal it. Looking over it at her, he takes a tiny bite to tease.

"That's a big carrot you have there," she coos. "Wanna share? I *love* big carrots."

Mel doesn't reply directly, but widens his stance and shifts his hips to one side as if his perch has become less comfortable. It's fall, not spring, but Mae isn't just another squirrel. She's far better proportioned than the other females, obsessed with love, and more deliberately provocative. Too bad she isn't to be trusted. She would make a bad partner, Mel grouses inwardly.

"They're good for you, have better vitamins than acorns," he informs her, as if it truly were a fact and the reason for his husbandry. "They help you at night."

"Oh, I've got something for that," Mae offers back.

"They're good for the eyes, I mean."

"And a lot more. How about we share that big carrot of yours?" Mae asks provocatively.

Yes, it's fall. It and the season to follow must be concluded before the renewal rituals that characterize spring will be manifest. Still, Mel's been aroused. Not every act, even those biological, need have a purpose.

"I know what big carrots like that can do," Mae says, exaggerating the seduction in her tone. "For your eyes, is that it? Then why don't you come up and see me?"

"I see you just fine," Mel tells her. He knows, instinctively, the way most real knowledge is held, that fall is the time to be putting on fat and not for making early babes that would starve during the barren winter. But then again ...

* * * * *

On the grass below, the family has decided it's time to leave.

"Nate?... Nathan!" his father yells from the car. "Don't just stand there making a face. Help your mother put what's left back in the basket."

*** *CHAPTER 2* ***

Nathan attempts one final menacing look then does as asked. The last bite of a sweet sandwich, the peanut butter thickly spread on white bread and warm from the sun, slips from his hand onto the picnic blanket. In a flash the two previously squabbling squirrels, which had been outflanked by the more bold one, scamper onto its rumpled edge. Unwilling to share, they engage in a brief tussle to decide which is going to claim ownership of the, in their view, abandoned treat.

"Go to the car," Marianne tells the children, as she firmly pulls up the blanket. This sends the bushy tailed combatants tumbling but also tips over the picnic basket. She has little reason to be fearful, but reason has nothing to do with it. The squirrels' sudden dash caught her off guard and instinct prevails. She repeats her motherly command in a louder voice. Before she can blink twice, the children are in the back seat and staring out through the closed window. Following close behind, she throws the blanket in a heap inside the trunk of their small car.

Meanwhile, the loser in the battle for the sweet leaving has turned its attention to the wicker basket, an old-fashioned one with two hinged lids. It senses that it holds yet more.

"Will you get the basket, please, Norman," Marianne requests of her husband, "before they tear it up?"

"I was about to," he says, one hand on the open passenger side door. "Should've put it in the trunk first."

**** CHAPTER 2 ****

Making noises and clapping his hands to dispel the squirrels as he approaches, he's surprised that the one sniffing at the basket's lid is unimpressed. It crouches but makes no move to run off. The father pulls up smartly on the side of the basket's handle, annoyed by the creature's bold attitude. Its lid opens so that a bag of cookies, invitingly unsealed, falls out upon the grass and is immediately targeted by the now not so cute scavenger. The startled father starts to reach down but pulls back when the previous squirrel returns to join in the competition. Neither of the furry adventurers seems afraid. Norman is beset with an unfamiliar choice of escalation versus retreat.

"Bold little shits," he growls. "Never enough? You want it all?"

Uncharacteristically for him, he pulls back his foot to provide a firm kick of encouragement. Visualizing his son's similar move earlier, he does not do so. Instead, the squirrels already at the thin bag's contents, he abandons the cookies and returns to the car. After investigating the interior of the basket, he latches its lid before setting it in the trunk. He looks back for a moment – his expression showing a mixture of puzzlement, annoyance, and incipient anger – then sits behind the wheel.

"You see that?" he rhetorically asks his wife. "They're definitely getting too used to people."

"I think they just don't like us," she replies. "We're not nearly as cute to them as they are to us. Or were."

"Maybe," Norman says.

"I don't think they're cute anymore," Victoria chimes in from the back seat. "They're scary."

"I'd just give 'em a kick. That'd teach 'em," Nathan boasts as he looks out through the back window at the receding vista. He wrinkles his incipiently squared off chin. "Next picnic, I'll bring my BB gun," he repeats.

"It's 'teach *them*', Nathan. Don't say 'teach-em.' That sounds sloppy," Marianne instructs him. She glances at the two older gentlemen who are watching them from a bench not too far off. She offers a small smile in their direction.

* * * * *

George Martino, about to lift his bony frame from the bench he's sharing with Brevan Shannon, has on the adult version of Nathan's expression.

"Look at that!" he exclaims. "They tried to jump in the basket."

"I saw." Shannon leans forward to get a last glimpse of the car driving off. "I don't think they bit anyone. Do you?"

"No, Goddamn 'em. But what's the difference?" Martino puts to his friend. "They would've if they could've. That's the damn point!"

"I wonder if they carry rabies?" Brevan asks of the space in front of him.

"Filthy vermin with filthy mouths, rabies or not. Every damn one of them."

Martino is angry out of proportion with the turn of events. It's as if he's making a special effort to be agitated, as if it were his picnic that was disturbed.

His mood carries over to his companion, who stands suddenly, puts both hands on his hips, sticks his chin in the air, much like the image on an old World War Two Italian rallying poster. He stares, with grim determination, up at the canopy of oaks. A Black Shirt Officer's Fez and bandolier would make the picture complete.

"It's the picnic people's own fault, if you want the solemn truth," he says ponderously and with the finality that comes from a lifetime of self-assurance without responsibility. "They think being nice and throwing treats is okay," he indicates the now distant vehicle and says. "So look what those bushy-tailed rats go ahead and do. Instead of enjoying what's given, they want to decide for themselves what's theirs and what's not. To hell with them. We'd be far better off being rid of them. I'm glad there's no limit on squirrels."

"Sure, open season all year 'round," George replies. "Still, there's just too many. As quick as they're taken more pop up. An endless supply it seems. All they must do, when they get active after the winter, is screw," he laughs.

"Nicely put, Professor Martino."

**** CHAPTER 2 ****

*   *   *   *   *

"Wow, as if Mel charging at the little girl wasn't bad enough," Sandy observes as the family leaves. "Those other two fools had to jump at their basket. That wasn't good."

"Was one of them Beryl again?" Caesar asks, rubbing graying cheeks with his forepaws. "Where did he come from? Doesn't he have enough stored in his hole up there already?"

"No, it wasn't Beryl. He'd already stuffed another acorn in his mouth and come back. It was Kiki and that Cody. She's the aggressive one. Cody just follows along, for the most part. I've never spent time with them. But, Beryl? No, he'll never have enough. That's the way he is. He'll never have enough of anything, I suppose," Sandy sighs. "Those other two were just taking advantage of an opportunity. Probably didn't think about what they were doing. Treats like that are tempting. They're softer and sweeter." Sandy rubs his paws over his snout then scratches behind one ear. "I do think, though, that those children didn't have to make such a big deal out of it and get their parents angry, too," he adds after further consideration. "We're just being squirrels."

"I know," Caesar replies. "Just being what we are.... To be fair, though, the two little ones were just being children and the parents were just looking out for them. Everyone puts those close to them at the top of the list. Someday, maybe this coming spring, you'll do the same, I wager. So, it's a matter of reasons and everyone has theirs."

*** *CHAPTER 2* ***

Sandy understands Caesar's point. After several springs, however, he's grown less interested in its prospects. The abstract now has more attraction to him than the concrete.

"Hey, M.T.," Sandy calls out, having spotted Beryl returning from his nest. He's glad for the diversion since Caesar tends to be too philosophical for him at times. "It's good you're sticking with acorns. Gobbling up cookies won't do your teeth any good. It'll just make you fat."

"Don't call me that," Beryl protests. "Anyway, that's the point now. Isn't it?"

"Why not 'M.T.'?" Sandy shoots back, ignoring the prescient observation. "Messy Tail Beryl is your name, isn't it?"

"No, just Beryl, snot-face."

"Oooh, got me there," Sandy says to his adjacent compatriot. "Put me in my place, for sure." Then, again to Beryl, he calls, "Messy Tail, Messy Tail. Too dumb to keep it out of your dump. What we know, you never learnt."

"Stop, Sandy," Caesar advises him. "He can't help it. Probably from being nearly killed by that bike when he was a pup."

"Pup, dumb pup. Now can't keep it up," the unheeding Sandy calls to Beryl.

"Pup, pup; dumb, dumb pup. He's the pup who can't keep it up," nearby Beater chatters in a plosive di- and trisyllabic refrain. Having repeated it with more syncopation to encourage a chorus of response from others scattered among the branches, he becomes the focus of Beryl's ire. The latter charges, but Beater, unsurprisingly, is nimbler. He leaps upward from limb to limb too quickly for Beryl to follow.

"You're too slow, M.T.," Twitch calls out.

Beryl turns back to challenge, gnashing his teeth to make certain the nearsighted Twitch will comprehend the threat even if he can't see it very well.

"How about I bite your ass," Beryl then tells him, despite that Twitch is innocent of any real complicity. He rears up when Jolie leaps down between them.

"Leave him, alone, Beryl," she says. It's not that she's bigger or faster or even more aggressive. It's that she's a she that gives Beryl pause. He bites the air a few times then claws his way up the rough bark of the oak's trunk and disappears.

"You didn't need to do that," Twitch says to her. "I can take care of myself. Sort of."

"Take what's left of that sticky bread stuff out of your mouth. I can't understand what you're saying."

He does so and repeats, exactly but more clearly, what he's just said.

"Sure, you can *sort of* take care of yourself. Sort of. One of these days, you're going to go too far and he or some other is going to hurt you."

"I didn't do anything. I'm a lover not a fighter," he protests, unsure whether his assertions will be taken literally and not confident that they should be.

"Well, don't get ahead of yourself. You're not either," Jolie says as she moves closer and blinks one big eye at him. "Not yet, anyway."

She stays silent while Twitch attempts to disambiguate her remark. Finally, she decides to confide in him.

"You're cute, Twitch. I haven't told you that before but you are. I like being with you. I've tried to make that obvious. But you haven't responded. Not even when ..." She hesitates and looks aside coyly.

Twitch's tails jerks more spasmodically. He stares back uncertainly at Jolie, whose light frame and smooth, shiny coat has always made her his favorite, albeit tentatively distant potential mate. In their world, being a lover absolutely means being a fighter.

"I ... I ..." he starts. "It's not that I'm afraid. I'm just not ready. I want to see more, explore more. I listen to Caesar and Sandy talk and know that there's so much that I *don't* know. Winter's almost here, Jolie. Then it'll be spring again. And then ..." Twitch sits more upright. Nervous and slightly embarrassed, he wishes he could better control the movements of his tail that so reveal his divided state of mind. What he should say and then do are dimly apparent to him but he cannot quite manage either. "I'm building a new, bigger nest up there." He nods upward, into the thinning canopy. "You and I can ... you and I will ... we'll have ... Forget it," he blurts out.

His painful lack of certainty disappoints but does not surprise Jolie. It's not the first time he's presented himself that way.

Sandy and Caesar have watched quietly from a distance.

"They're a couple, it seems to me," Caesar observes. "We'll know come spring.... They'd better decide. We don't get that many seasons."

"Just what we need, more twitchies to amuse the humans," Sandy sighs.

"No accounting for taste, Sandy. Nor couplings. An odd pair, but they do seem to be fond of each other."

"Well, he can't see very well, but she can. What does a cute little scuria like Jolie want with a reject like Twitch?"

"Do I hear a little jealousy in the forest," Caesar teases him.

This is enough to close off the topic.

Sandy folds his paws against his chest and looks down.

CHAPTER THREE

After putting aside their consideration of Twitch and Jolie, of what may or may not result from their alliance, Caesar and Sandy stare down at the flattened grass where the humans had their picnic. They seem to be reading some significance into the small drama they've just witnessed.

"Can you please tell me what they think they're doing?" Sandy asks of Caesar, his older and therefore wiser friend. "First Mel scares the little girl, then those other two, Kiki and Cody, steal cookies and try to jump in their basket. Are they too stupid to realize how much bigger the humans are than we and what that means? Did you see how those men on the bench took it in? I've seen that look before, when others of their sort were marching through the forest with their long guns. Never here, as far as I know. But they wouldn't think twice about stepping on our necks or putting out traps or poisoned food if they felt a need."

"They're bigger, sure. And meaner. But they're mean at a distance, most of them, not close up," Caesar observes. "They consider themselves civilized. They're used to negotiating and having other people fight their battles. They're not good at just plain reacting. It frightens them, actually. But you're right. When they've had time to think about it, that's when to watch out. Then come the traps. And I don't mean the ones for capturing and relocating. The traps that kill. They have poisons. And guns, too. Even if clever enough to avoid the rest, it's hard to scamper away from shotguns and rifles."

"So why did Cody and Kiki take the chance of stealing from that picnic?" Sandy swivels his head this way and that, as if seeking a better view.

"Why? You need to know Why?" Caesar scoffs. The gray streaks in the fur near his eyes lend an aura of puzzlement tinged with worry to his steady gaze. "The Why is that they wanted what was in the basket."

"Obviously, dimwits. You don't see an open spread like that very often," a voice from an adjacent branch calls out. "I wish I hadn't gone back up and been so far away myself."

"Open spread? It wasn't open." Caesar isn't impressed by Beryl's know-it-all tone. "The basket wasn't open until Kiki jumped on it," he informs him.

"It wasn't latched. It was going to fall open, anyway, as soon as the man tried to pick it up."

After Beryl has thus framed the issue in the squirrels' favor, he crouches and clicks his teeth lightly.

"You're sure of that, Beryl?" Caesar puts to him. "The man wasn't just going to pick it up and go on his way?"

"Certainly, I'm sure," Beryl says firmly.

"You're always sure, about everything, aren't you M.T.?" snickers Sandy"

"Don't call me that, I said. I don't like it."

"I know you don't," replies Sandy, punctuating this with a suggestive sniff.

Beryl shifts back onto his rear legs and lets his forepaws dangle in front of him. He does his best to keep his tail upright, as is the norm for most squirrels, now that it has become a focus of attention. He rejects the nickname, M.T., because it stands for "Messy Tail." An often pompous, yet happy to follow-the-leader squirrel, he suffers the dual misfortune of weak hindquarters and a less than thoughtful nature. He's frequently been seen to drag his tail over his own ... well, his own excrement. If he pays attention he can avoid the embarrassment, but that's precisely the problem. He's generally more concerned with the impression he wants to make rather than the one he's actually making. That's a common trait among otherwise unimpressive creatures.

*** *CHAPTER 3* ***

Sandy decides not to elaborate upon his tease. It's too familiar and is losing its edge. He instead tries to make amends by engaging Beryl in a dialogue.

"Did you see the little girl almost start to cry?" Sandy asks. "She was trying to be nice. Not like those others with their rocks and sticks. Or those pesky little dogs."

"I did," Beryl tells him. "It wasn't smart of Mel to rush at her. But then, he isn't."

Caesar and Sandy blink their black eyes.

"He perked up that other pair's nerve, though, didn't he?" Sandy poses.

"Stupidity needs company," Caesar adds.

"What's with the stupidity?" Beryl demands. "You don't like free snacks? Kiki and what's his name weren't stupid. Besides, like you said, it was Mel who started it, by running in and grabbing that damn carrot. He was one who first scared the little one, got everyone hyper." He looks down toward the base of their tree, no longer certain that he should have hesitated. "I've seen that family here before. I think they recognized me."

"Recognized you??? You're an ..." Caesar chooses not to finish what was to be an unkind observation. "We look alike to them," he instead explains calmly. "All the little girl's going to remember is that one squirrel seemed about to bite her, not *which* one and –"

"That was Mel's fault," Beryl interrupts to repeat. "He started it and –"

*** *CHAPTER 3* ***

"Okay, okay," Sandy, in turn, stops him to say. "They were wrong but not as wrong as Mel, so they were relatively right? Is that your point?"

Beryl's small jaws work side to side. He doesn't often attempt logical analysis, even the silly kind, and isn't sure how to respond to this second critique.

"Well, something like that" he eventually attempts. "Yes. It's all relative." He seems to feel he's added sufficient clarification to the discussion and turns away.

"And what the man is going to remember," Caesar resumes," is that two squirrels tried to get into his picnic basket. He's not going to care which ones next time he comes."

"The same goes for you," Twitch hears from Jolie, who's been sitting behind him on a nearby branch. "That was shameful."

They've attended to but felt no need to join the discussion among the other three.

"Why me? The little girl offered it," Twitch complains, in the pouty manner of one accustomed to being chastised. He presses against the top of his nose with the back of one forepaw, as if pushing back a pair of spectacles, which his large eyes filling out what, even for a squirrel, looks to be a small head seems to suggest. "I came back up after and just watched. What did I do?"

"Nothing," she replies with a slow nod, which seems to add an additional dimension to her admonition

"Oh, I see," Twitch says, with a slow nod back. "You're saying I should've scrambled down and played hero. Ever see the teeth on that Mel? He's always greedy for the soft food. Pretty soon his incisors will be too long for him to close his mouth. He already looks like a predator. No wonder the little girl was scared and dropped the carrot."

"Well, you should've done something."

"I did. I scowled at him when he came back, to let him know he shouldn't be doing that."

"Wow. Scowled. Aren't you the brave one," Jolie mocks. "That's not much."

"Oh, so that's not much?" Twitch snorts back, blinking his huge eyes rapidly. "To you maybe. But it was plenty for me."

"What about those other two?" Jolie challenges.

"What about them? Suppose I jumped down there and tried to chase them off. Then what? The man was already angry. It would've just made him angrier. And Kiki has a nasty bite herself. I'm glad it's just Cody that she's always fighting with. I wouldn't want to mess with her. Anyway, none of them down there would have known what I was meaning to do if I had jumped in. They would've thought I was after the basket myself.... Do I look like a super hero to you?"

"No," Jolie snickers, "you most certainly do not. That's a definite no," she adds as she hops down a branch to be closer to Sandy and Caesar. "That's not how we should be behaving," she says to them jointly. "Is it?"

Before the two more senior squirrels can reply there's a small commotion above them. It's Mae scampering down from high in the canopy, her claws gripping the bark of the oak. Mel, slower in his descent, is not far behind.

The ever mobile Beater, who persistently presumes that others are entertained by watching him, pauses his gyrations and eyes them as they pass.

"Kissy kissy," he chatters, eliciting not a mote of response.

"Good for you?" Mel calls ahead once Mae has taken up a position on a branch.

"Not bad, for the season," she offers him. "Come see me again in the spring. A good squirrel is hard, too."

Mel blinks a few times then looks down. Nothing remains of the picnic.

"Crap. They've gone. I'm hungry now; could use a snack."

"You're always thinking about food," Mae tells him. "After."

Beater, up on his haunches, bobs his head and works his jaws in mock jealousy. He simultaneously thrusts his hips from side to side.

"That didn't take long," Beater snidely remarks. He retreats when Mel feints in his direction. "I guess it never does. We're squirrels," he then observes sarcastically. "Mel and Mae, sitting in a tree," he sings, since Mel is a safe distance away, "K I S S I N G."

"Food and sex," says Twitch. "That's all Mel thinks about, the dumb-ass. I wish it were that simple."

"It really is. But you're the dumber-ass," Beater smirks. "Food and sex *is* all there is.... Twitch in a tree, has the hots for Jolie," he then says in rhythm with his bops and hops. "Twitch in a tree and can't do what he see."

"Why is everyone picking on me? Mel was the one who started it," Twitch again complains.

Sandy and Caesar exchange glances.

"We've got bigger problems," Sandy says to Caesar, knowing it didn't need to be said for the wise squirrel's benefit, but wanting the others to hear.

"We do," Caesar agrees. "And it's only going to get worse if we behave like that. We can't be trying to take what they don't want to give. I'm more concerned now than ever I was." He looks from one to the other of the nearby squirrels. "Having these huge trees to live in is a lot better than being in the forest. These acorns aren't like those from the smaller trees; they're fatter and they taste better." He pauses to detect any signs of agreement before continuing. "We even get small treats from the humans sometimes. That's always a nice change. I think it's kind of fun to interact with them. Like a change of scene. It wouldn't be the same in the forest. And it wouldn't be as safe. There are plenty of bigger, stronger creatures that would love to make a meal of *us*."

"That's the key," Sandy agrees. "We have to make the humans want to share with us. They always have more than they need when they come here. We just need to make it fun for them so they will."

"I can dance," Beater offers then proceeds to do. "That gets their attention."

Caesar briefly looks his way but continues to address his comments to Sandy.

"I'm still concerned. I didn't like the way those men on the bench watched us. I've the feeling, from the looks on their faces and the way they waved their hands, that they weren't having nice thoughts about us. I can't help but think they felt we were in the wrong, that we were doing what we shouldn't. If we're not careful they'll chase us away from here, chase us into the forest, maybe. They're much more powerful than we."

"Like hell," Mel states in a loud voice as he approaches. He's put aside his interest in Mae for the moment. "Down there, maybe, but not up here. They need to share. We can be like mosquitoes and pester the hell out of them until they do. They can't catch us."

"That's a stupid, stupid thing to say, Mel," Caesar says. "You know what happens to mosquitoes, don't you?"

"What?" Mel snaps.

"They get slapped."

"So, are all the mosquitoes gone?" Mel asks before answering himself. "No. Can't get rid of us either. They'll learn soon enough that they have to share."

"He's hopeless," Sandy observes softly. "He's got a one track ... Excuse me, I mean a two track mind."

"These are our trees, too," Mel insists. "Don't forget that. We've earned the right."

"Just living here doesn't make them ours," Caesar points out.

"Well, you can't make things different if you don't try," Mel states obstinately.

Sandy really doesn't disagree.

"You've got a point, I suppose," he says. "Making a difference does start with trying to do something. Talk is a lame substitute for action."

Having heard Sandy's similar thoughts in the past, Caesar anticipates what he's about to suggest.

"And that difference," Caesar explains, "can be nothing like what you set out to make." The elder squirrel has a broader and therefore a somewhat different view at the ready. "To every action there's a reaction. We mature squirrels need to act better, set examples for the younger ones. We should make a point of being pleasant and fun so that they, the humans, are glad that we're here."

"I see. We're supposed to run around, be furry clowns, and take what we're given," Mel grumbles, with a trace of bitterness. "To hell with that. They set out that tasty food for themselves and drop bits on the ground. They always bring more than they can eat. They intend for us to go after it and ..." He looks down at where the picnic blanket was, as if a few tidbits might yet have been overlooked. "They're showing off, is what they're doing. Showing off that they have more than they need and have the time to just come out here and lay around like there's never going to be a winter."

"That, my fine furry friend, sounds like the definition of envy to me. Are you jealous?" Caesar asks him. "You'd like to be human and have their worries?"

"We should go down there when they get up from their blankets," Mel growls. "Then they'll leave it all. We can pester them, jump in and out so they have to pay more attention to us than to their silly picnic. Keep them from enjoying it."

"Oh, stop. What would that prove?" Caesar turns his back to Mel. Starting along the branch, he adds, "Then they'd bring out the shotguns for sure." He lets out a deep sigh, one of experience tempered by age.

"Look, Mel," Sandy tries to offer, "we have our place and they have theirs. They come out here for a picnic. They want to relax, play, smell the grass, and stare up at the sky. So what? These are their oak trees."

"How the hell are they theirs?" Mel persists in asking. "If we didn't stick acorns in the ground they wouldn't have their damn oaks."

"We?" Caesar calls back. "See any oak saplings here, Mel? Do you have any idea how long it took for these oaks to get so big?... No, I'll bet you don't. They've been here for so many seasons after seasons I can't even conceive of it. Maybe, even, they were here before any of us." He sits on his haunches, staring up along the oak's solid trunk into its canopy of leaves. After a few quiet moments he turns back to Mel. "Ruining what they want to do," he observes, "doesn't give us anything."

"Exactly," says Sandy. "At best, they won't come for their picnics. They won't come here, and we'll have to settle for acorns and acorns and more acorns."

"Well, that might not be so bad," Caesar comments thoughtfully. "The junk they eat isn't good for us. Acorns are much healthier. And they last through winter without getting moldy and worse, like their scraps do."

"Bah," Beryl chimes in. "The humans enjoy what they eat and we could, too."

"Right. I say run up and pretend to bite them," Mel asserts. "Chatter and gnash our teeth so that leave everything and run off. Then *we'd* have the picnic!"

The idea seems to suit him but no one else. Sandy and Caesar crouch low, staring at him balefully.

"What?" Mel exclaims. "There's something wrong with that?"

"Great idea, Mel. Snap at 'em, bite at 'em; jump at 'em an' frighten 'em," Beater facetiously rhymes, hopping about.

Acknowledging neither the suggestion nor the juvenile display that it inspired, Caesar stares at the belligerent Mel.

*** *CHAPTER 3* ***

"Great idea? Bah. It's one of the stupidest ideas I've ever heard. You're as bad as Beryl, here. You know that? Lots of noise with very little inside."

"Annoy them once in a while, then," Mel persists. "Gnash our teeth and jump around when they stare. Startle them so they'll forget to eat what they've brought."

"And who says they would –?" Caesar starts but is interrupted by Sandy.

"Amazing, Mel. Here I thought your first idea was so bad, like Caesar said, that you couldn't top it. Wow, was I wrong. Look, you're not going to make them afraid except for maybe the first time, when they're surprised. You're only going to make them angry. And what do you think will happen then? Think about the tools they have. They'll scour the woods *and* here with their shotguns to kill us. Put down poison, set traps, and send the dogs out. They'd get rid of us, that's what."

"Let them try," inserts Beryl, who thus far has had little to say. "We can hide, we can scamper. Have you ever seen one of them catch one of us? No. Even if they get close, they back off at the last moment when they see our teeth. There's no way they can get rid of us. Not unless they cut down the entire forest. There are too many of us. They'll have to ruin it for themselves before they can ruin it for us."

"Self-centered foolishness," Caesar gnashes out. "You've both gone acorns, I'm afraid. Making the humans angry will only make them vicious."

"Then be fun-fun and funny," Beater sing-songs. "It'll turn out sunny" He strikes a pose and wrinkles the fur behind his nose.

"It's getting to be time for long naps," Caesar says, trying to ignore Beater's antics. "It's nearly winter and my guess is that it's going to be a long, cold one." He shakes his head and stares at Sandy for confirmation. Then, repeating basically what he had said earlier to Mel and Beryl, he says, "They have ways to deal with us that we haven't seen yet, you can be sure. Ways that we can't even imagine. We'd be much better off enhancing their lives than antagonizing them."

As usual, Caesar is too wise for his audience.

"Well," Beryl starts, erecting his tail and waving it about, "I'd just as soon have this place to myself – to *our*selves, I mean."

"Stinky," Twitch says and scampers away.

"Yeah, Messy Tail," growls Mel, "Stop waving it about."

Beryl drops down onto his forepaws and shows his teeth to Mel. He jumps forward a foot or so, then retreats. It's a standoff. They and Beater move off in their different directions with nothing resolved. Another night is coming and it's time to settle into their nests. Winter's chill will ensure that they spend more time there.

Mel feels a familiar but untimely agitation, a need for company and perhaps more. He looks about for Mae. He sees her, several branches above, close to another squirrel, one unfamiliar to him and with a coat of a different shade. Inwardly, his mood suddenly cools. Mae is, he knows, a tease, but it would be better if she were more discerning.

"Slut," Mel snaps as he scoots past Beryl.

The latter has no idea of the significance or intent of the insult. Concluding – quite correctly since Mel doesn't make eye contact – that the reference isn't meant for him, he takes it simply as more evidence of Mel's prickly nature.

Jolie, also looking to nest as the darkness deepens, hops up branch by branch with Twitch not far behind.

"Wait, Jolie," he pleads. "I'm sorry about the picnic people." He blinks his big eyes then squints up into the green gloom. "Sorry.... Wait up."

"That doesn't take it away," Jolie throws back to him. "Feeling sorry doesn't take what you did away and it doesn't make it okay."

"Why are you so upset about this?" Twitch wants to know. "Nothing really happened."

"Is that what you think? Just because they didn't throw something at you or send a dog to chase after you, you think it was right to pester them?"

"I didn't pester. And they didn't have a dog."

"Tshhh," hisses an exasperated Jolie. "It's what's going to happen in the future that I'm talking about. Caesar is smart. If he's worried then we should be, too. You, we doing things like that is a bad thing. The humans are going to remember that the next time they come, if they do. Maybe they'll tell other people and it'll change their minds about us. Small things, like what you did, have wings, Twitch. They fly around and make big messes, like pigeons."

"That's kinda poetic, Jolie. I like that," he says.

"Poetic?" Jolie stares at Twitch and lets her annoyance melt. "You're not getting my meaning one bit," she says more softly, "so just forget it. Good night. But think about it."

Twitch follows her for a bit, but her pace and subsequently ignoring his playful yet pleading chatter cause him to lag behind. He turns and scampers off in a different direction.

Side by side and quiet for a long time, Sandy and Caesar haven't heard what transpired between Jolie and Twitch. But they've watched and can guess.

"I have the feeling," the former says, "that Jolie understands what's going on more than most of us."

"Females usually do," Caesar remarks. "They have more time to think about things and more things to think about. Having kits tends to make what the future will be a more pressing concern, I would think."

"That makes sense," Sandy says. "But just stewing about it doesn't accomplish much."

"No. You're right. It makes it seem like you're doing something while you're really not. Still, I'm afraid we've a lot to worry about," Caesar sighs. "You need to think about that. Soon it'll be your turn to carry the worry and give advice."

*** *CHAPTER 3* ***

Sandy examines his friend, his mentor. He takes in the gray streaks in Caesar's coat, the very dark stains on his teeth, the heavy body that has become more fat than muscle.

"You're showing your age, in more ways than one," Sandy tells him.

"I'm tired, you mean? You're right. I am. As I said, soon you'll have to take over. The youngsters will need all the help and advice they can get. But, I hate to say, if Mel and Beryl are any indication, they're being pointed in the wrong direction."

"Well, then you need to tell us what to do, exercise your authority as an elder. Don't let on that you're tired or discouraged. You know what we need to do and not do, sure, but you've got to find a way to get that across, to enforce it even. Authority comes from wisdom not force."

"That's the trouble, Sandy. Here," Caesar observes, "just like in the forest, it may be the other way around."

CHAPTER FOUR

"No, no, no," Mayor Hays Bales is saying into the telephone. It's a land line. On the other end is one of the few people who use it to call him – his wife, Maya. "I can't do another dinner out. Just make –" He grimaces and eyes his political aide, Brevan Shannon. "Anything, Maya, anything. Simple, very simple. Very simple is just fine with me.... Yes, a very simple salad.... I've been –" He relaxes the handset away from his ear for a few seconds then resumes. "We've been eating too much rich food. Too much. It's bad for us.... Yes, that'll be fine.... Maya, I need to go. I've got people arriving in a few moments. Important people.... Yes.... Yes, I'll be home in time for the news." He hangs up the phone slowly, deliberately, concluding with a small flourish. "I like going out, just not every damn night," he explains to Shannon.

*** *CHAPTER 4* ***

Mayor Bales' profile has grown to be more than adequate over the past few years. Having a bit of a paunch, which he manages to keep less obvious via expensive suits, is part of looking like a mayor, of indeed being Mayor. He's been blessed with a big head and eyes not in need of corrective lenses – something that many in public life, whether entertainer or politician, find advantageous. Because his shock of light-colored hair is prone to be unruly, he keeps a coarse comb, small hand mirror, and traveler-sized can of hair spray in his desk. With short arms and short legs sprouting from an overly large body, his overall stature hasn't prevented some of his detractors from likening him to a dwarf. Mayor Bales manages to turn this to his favor, however, by projecting that the critique stems from jealous spite and has no basis. He, his aide, and his staff are quite adept in conveying that he's physically and administratively a giant of a man.

"That's what's nice about being a bachelor. I can do any damn thing I please," Brevan states.

"You think so?"

"Well, anything I please when I'm not here, anyway."

Brevan Shannon, the mayor's politically adept aide-de-camp, is not nearly so concerned about his personal appearance. Also large bodied, he presents a ruddy complexion that suggests overexertion burdened with intemperance. In dramatic contrast to his boss, however, he's neither a neat nor a sensible dresser. Always in jackets and slacks that seem to have been cut for someone even larger, he gives the appearance, at best, of having recently lost weight or, at worst, of being unconcerned with the impression he leaves. As if by design, the distinction between the front office and back office aspirations of the two men could not, therefore, be more evident.

"Are they late?" Shannon asks.

Mayor Bales takes a slow look at his watch.

Almost simultaneously the intercom on his big desk comes to life.

"Mister Putter and Mister Steerman are here."

"Send them in, Sylvia."

Bales gets up and motions for Shannon to position another chair next to the empty one already next to his. He had expected only one to arrive to talk about the oak harvest.

He extends his hand to his guests.

"Hello, Mister Putter. Nice to see you again. You remember my aide, Brevan Shannon."

"Of course I do. How are you, Mister Shannon?" He smiles and nods, precisely as he has received. "And thank you, of course, Mister Mayor, for taking time from your busy schedule to see us. This is Thadeus Steerman. He's in charge of the selection and cutting."

"Glad to meet you, Mister Steerman," Hays Bales offers civilly as they conclude shaking hands. "You and your crews have always done neat, professional work. Very professional," he extends to the thin, woodsy looking fellow whose complexion suggests much sun and exposure to the elements. Except for the fact that he's wearing no tie, he's a thinner version of Brevan Shannon.

"Yup. I try to do that," Steerman responds.

Bales pokes a button on his intercom. "Bring us that fresh pot of coffee, Sylvia, please."

"Nothing for me, thanks," says Putter.

Steerman shakes his head to indicate a silent second.

"Never mind, Sylvia. We're fine as we are," he instructs, via the box on his desk, before sitting. "So. How can I help you?"

"Well, Mister Mayor, as you know, of course, we have to plan ahead. It takes months to select, harvest, and properly season the oak wood. It seems that what we cut last year wasn't nearly enough. We had to buy additional stock elsewhere to meet our customers' needs. In particular the home furnishings people. Supplies of oak stock have gotten thin, even for trim and flooring materials. We retained enough rough cut and scrap to meet that. But the furniture people are more interested in the heartwood." He smiles at Bales and his aide. "We're fortunate that Putter Lumber has built a fine reputation. We've always striven to meet our customers' needs both in quality *and* quantity."

"Then you'll want to contract for more trees this year?" Bales asks.

"Bigger," Steerman states.

"Excuse me?" The Mayor responds.

**** CHAPTER 4 ****

"The issue, Mister Mayor," Putter starts, "is that we need to acquire more of the bigger trees. Many more. The bigger the tree –"

"The older the tree, the more heartwood it'll yield," Steerman inserts. "Sapwood's fine for flooring and such, but heartwood's what the furniture people need. Tighter grain. It takes a much finer finish."

"That sums it up nicely," Putter says, turning his steady smile from the speaker to the mayor. "In a relatively young tree, you see, most of its cross section is sapwood. It's what passes the nutrients and water up the trunk for growth, for the leaves and such. Over time, as the tree grows, it gets taller, of course, but also the trunk gets bigger, thicker. It grows in diameter. New wood overlays the old. The old wood changes, dies in a sense, and become harder. The interior layers then are more important for the trees' structural support than for, let's just say, than for its nutrition."

"That's the heartwood. What furniture makers want," Steerman tersely but redundantly inserts.

"I see," Mayor Bales replies, although actually not quite sure of the point being made.

Putter, an experienced and knowledgeable negotiator, perceives this dissonance.

"The point is this, Mister Mayor," he leans forward to state. "We need to be more selective." He glances at Steerman so as to validate his particular utility. "Thadeus is a good judge of old growth oak. And that's what we require. More old growth stock. The younger trees have been fine for flooring and trim oak. If kilned –"

"Dried, in a kiln, Mister Bales," Steerman clarifies.

"Yes, when dried properly, in a kiln, even the sap wood will serve for that," Putter continues on. "It's the older trees, of course, that are going to be bigger and will yield more heartwood, in addition to a good proportion of flooring and trim wood. As I've said, we see a very lucrative opportunity in providing highest quality oak heartwood to furniture makers."

"Craftsmen?"

"Not craftsmen so much, Mister Shannon," Putter turns slightly to reply. "They're not a big market for us. There aren't enough of them and their needs are too small. I'm talking, of course, about the commercial, high end furniture and cabinetry manufactures. They can't seem to get enough old growth white oak and will pay well above market price for high quality material." He leans back in his chair and taps one of its arms lightly and rhythmically with his finger.

"Well, then, I imagine there must be quite a few large oaks out there, very large. Perhaps they're deeper into the forest. Is it access that you're concerned about?" Mayor Bales turns his face briefly to Shannon. "I'm sure we can extend your permit to include additional access roads, as long as they're not permanently paved or anything like that. Where there hasn't been much logging, I'm sure you'll find older, bigger oaks."

"Right. There's no problem with that," Shannon agrees. "As long as it doesn't materially affect recreational use. People understand that local jobs and income are important, too. We can make sure the ecology folks are satisfied. A few 'Special Reports' in the newspaper and on TV should do it. We can make the case that those very far-in parts of the forest are –"

"Not enough old growth," interrupts the laconic Steerman.

"What Mister Steerman means to say, gentlemen," Putter says, "is that the forested areas around Oakville consist of haphazard natural growth, with lots of saplings. They're densely packed, for the most part, so they don't grow that big in the first place. And most of the harvestable trees are relatively young. It seems that, in the past, they'd been cut for years without any regulation. The trees we've been taking are less than a half-century old, with trunks not much more than about a foot in diameter, even in the relatively remote stands."

"Can't get much heartwood planking from them, even if flat-sawn. Nearly nothing wide enough if quarter-sawn, which is better."

Putter gestures for Steerman to not add further detail.

"What we mean to say is simply that we want to locate a source of high quality, old growth oak. That would give us the, say, twenty or twenty-four inch logs we need to supply our furniture fabricator customers." Putter removes his glasses and slips them into the upper pocket of his dark, faintly striped designer suit.

"But, as I suggested, if you go deeper into the forest, won't you find those older and bigger trees?" Bales inquires.

"I've looked," Steerman tells them with a negative head-shake.

"No, that's not the opportunity we're thinking about, Mister Mayor." Putter extends and spreads out his finger tips, tapping all but the outlier pinkies together as he gathers his thoughts. "And let's not be so formal, Hays. We've done business before." He looks at the intercom box on the desk and raises his eyebrows.

Bales is quick to pick up on the request. He pulls the old fashioned instrument closer, reaches behind, and unplugs a cable.

"Yes, Leon, we have," he says. "There's no need to be formal and there's no need to be shy. No need. What is it that you're asking?"

"Every time we've come to Oakville to finalize a timber contract I've had occasion to admire those outstanding old oaks in your park. They must be well more than a century old."

"The Founders Oaks? Yes, at least a hundred and fifty or more years old. Very, very old. We're quite sure a few are from the original plantings of two centuries ago." Bales says this with a mixture of pride and rising interest. "That's when Oakville was first settled."

**** CHAPTER 4 ****

This is as far as Mayor Bales intends to go. There's no need nor, he senses, wish to go into the history of his town, of who founded it, of when, or of why.

"I measured one at one hundred twenty inches around," Steerman admits, exuding admiration meant to mask his opportunism. "That's about a yard in diameter, and means probably an –"

"Really? I've never noticed," Shannon interjects.

"– which means an oak well over a hundred, maybe a hundred *and fifty* years old," the thin man energetically concludes. "And it's not even the biggest out there," he makes a point of adding.

"Well, that's not surprising, in view of how those trees came to be," Mayor Bales then has the opportunity to remark. "They've been there, in Oakville, virtually from the time if its first settlement."

He glances at his aide. Starting to catch up with the drift of the conversation, Shannon silently nodes assent.

"So, Hays, what would it take to receive your approval to harvest a few of those large oak trees. There are hundreds in the park. We could select some that are, let us say, so diseased or so old as to have become dangerous."

"That's not my decision to make. They're covered by the city charter you realize, Leon," Bales tells him cautiously.

"Of course, of course. I realize that," Putter soothes. "But, you could get that changed, couldn't you? Get a waiver through your City Council?" This, accompanied by Putter's unblinking contact with the mayor's eyes, is obviously more serial suggestion than query. "I think you can foresee how this could be quite beneficial to you."

Shannon purses his lips upon absorbing Putter's comments.

"For Oakville, I mean to say," Putter goes on, "of course. A substantial sum is anticipated and already budgeted. No doubt, Hays, there are worthwhile civic projects that lack only the necessary funds to get underway," he concludes stiffly, still smiling.

"I understand, Leon. I understand," Mayor Bales coos. "I'm in sympathy with your suggestion. Yes, very sympathetic. There are a number of items, very important items that the city's been putting off for budgetary reasons." Mayor Bales stands and walks around to his visitors, who rise to again shake his offered hand. "I'm glad you've gotten right to the point. Very glad. But I don't think we should pursue it further at this precise moment. We need first to determine how best to get this done." Mayor Bales returns Putter's unctuous smile. "Yes, that needs to be defined.... For the city," he adds. "Let's do this. Brevan and I will see that this is presented at the next City Council meeting. I'll get back with you after that and discuss your suggestion in more detail, much more. We can define the particulars at that time."

There's a knock on the door, which is followed by Sylvia's entrance.

*** CHAPTER 4 ***

"I'm sorry, Mayor Bales. Something seems to have happened with your intercom. Did you need me for anything?"

"Ah, yes, Sylvia," Bales says after a look back at his desk. "I see what happened. I seem to have unplugged it when moving it to one side. But no, there's nothing. Thank you. We had a bid on a new telephone system that would replace that old, old relic," he then addresses to Putter and Steerman, "but couldn't fit it into our budget this year. Next year, perhaps. Yes, next year's." Again addressing Sylvia, he asks, "Did I have a call?"

"No, sir. I just wanted to be sure everything was in order."

"Thank you. Yes, everything is fine, just fine. These gentlemen were just leaving."

His hand resting lightly on Putter's upper arm, he has them follow Sylvia into the reception area and bids them goodbye.

"In a few days then," he repeats to the exiting pair before closing the door. Back by his desk, Bales extends one hand to rest it on the inactive intercom. "What do you think, Brevan? Could we get that through?"

"We'd have to have good reason. People love the big trees in that park."

"I bet most don't pay any attention to them, really. They – the trees – are just there. They're taken for granted." Bales stands silent for a moment before he takes the chair next to Shannon. "What's your retirement fund looking like these days?" he asks. "Mine's been soft since last the last hiccup. Very soft. Very soft."

"Mine could use a boost, sure," his aide admits. "A fraction more's always better than a fraction less.... Any idea how much he might be inclined to do?"

"He sweetened last year's contract very, very nicely. He'd probably be willing to do more, a lot more for what he's asking now. We'll have to tease him a bit, 'of course.'" Bales chuckles lightly at his imitation of the man's manner of speaking.

"I don't understand that heartwood and sapwood business."

"I certainly don't, and I don't care to try." Mayor Bales pauses, looks down at his hands then up. "I didn't want to hear about it. If it's important to him, it'll be very lucrative for us. Very lucrative."

"Well, like I said, Hays, more is always better than less. Especially this close to retirement."

"We'll talk about it later. At the club, perhaps. Yes. We need a reason, a good, good reason to get the Council on board. That's primary. That's the key. If we get this worked out, it could be a big, big win for the city. A very substantially generous win. Don't you think so?" Bales asks.

Shannon replies with a sly smile that perfectly matches that of his boss.

The Mayor holds up his hands.

"One or two more terms is all I'm going to want," he claims. "Maybe not even that, if this goes well." Bales pulls the hand mirror from a drawer of his desk, to verify that his sturdy coif of straw-colored hair is rigidly in place, then runs a palm lightly over his temple. "I think we should meet with Marcus soon." With this, Bales reaches behind the intercom and pushes the cable back in.

"Yes, ASAP," Brevan agrees. "But let's not be too direct. He's very serious about being on the City Council."

"I know. He's a thinker, poor guy. Always thinking; always thinking. Yes, yes, we need to get him on board. Are you free for lunch tomorrow?"

"Sure, as long as it's on your tab." Brevan Shannon pats his waist as he lifts his bulk from the chair. "I'll even put on a fresh shirt."

"That's a good idea," Bales smiles back, "a very good idea. I'll phone Epps this evening and fill him in."

* * * * *

The Founders Club is the most prestigious, the uniquely prestigious, in fact, setting in Oakville. It's on the edge of Oak Park and has a dining room with an open sun porch that has a fine view of its oak trees but is sufficiently far from the play area to be undisturbed by its occupants. Mayor Bales and Shannon Brevan have already reduced their beverages by half by the time Marcus Epps joins them.

*** *CHAPTER 4* ***

"Have something to drink, Marcus."

"Well ... I don't know," he responds to the mayor's invitation. "It is kind of early." He looks at his watch. "What are you having? Iced tea?"

"You see any ice, Marcus? Bourbon, neat," Brevan announces.

"A scotch," Bales says over him, signaling the waiter. "It *is* past noon."

Epps lifts one hand and, with the back of his fingers, scratches at the loose flesh under his chin. The sparsely hirsute wattle, matched by an overall sagging countenance, a sharp, prominent nose, and somewhat bulging eyes, gives him a reptilian appearance. Some call him – not to his face, certainly – Councilman Gecko. When making a point or when thinking about doing so, however, he'll often elevate his chin and stretch out his wrinkled neck more like a turtle emerging from its shell.

"I'd like a ... a bourbon and water, please," Epps requests of the hovering, dark-skinned man without looking up.

Bales leads the conversation into innocuous pleasantries while they wait for Epps to be served then says "Cheers" and sips his scotch. Epps takes a substantial swallow, then another, so that he quickly catches up to the others in diminishing his drink. Adept at protocol and familiar with lubricating negotiation, Bales remains on a casual tack as they peruse the menu, order their lunch, and start on a second drink. Their salads taken away and well into their entrees, Bales glances at his aide before exploring the reason for taking lunch together.

"What are your thoughts, Marcus?" he puts to the ever serious Councilman.

"Well ... You said they want to harvest some of those on this next time around." Epps motions across the porch at the Founders Oaks.

"Thin them out a bit, actually," Shannon says. "I think it's fair to say that needs to be done."

"Yes," Bales adds, "we've been neglecting that. Not wise, not wise."

After receiving an acknowledging nod from his aide, Bales proceeds to outline the issue as had earlier been introduced in his office, focusing on the need for, rather than the potential monetary benefits of such a course.

"A few might be looking ... looking a little weak," Epps eventually replies. "But treatments, like with fertilizer and sprays, should take care of that. You really think some have to be cut down?"

"No, not have to, exactly. But to take out some would be beneficial, very beneficial, for the others. That's what Putter's arborist, Steerman, said," Bales states, being deliberately indirect while elevating the latter man's qualifications.

"Well ... What was wrong with the previous contracts? They seemed happy to pay for logging the forest.... There's plenty of oak wood still out there," he inserts into his pause before anyone else speaks.

"For flooring and trim lumber, sure," says Shannon, "but the Putter people need bigger logs. He has customers clamoring for furniture grade wood, heartwood he calls it."

"From the older of the Founders Oaks," Bales feels it's time to insert. "Those that are perhaps too old, that are no longer right for Oak Park and should be culled." He glances at his aide. "Some are very, very large and would yield a much higher fraction of the heartwood they want."

"The Founders Oaks," Epps starts, again indicating the nearby trees still showing the warm tones of fall, "are what make the park special..... They're what make Oakville special, in many ways. Isn't that right?"

"There's no plan to harvest all of them, Marcus. Just a few. Just a few. Some that won't be missed," Bales says earnestly. "Walk around out there. You'll see how many of those oaks look like they're failing."

Shannon Brevan adds a confident nod to validate the reasonableness of the mayor's misstatement.

"What are they offering?" Epps leans forward to ask quietly.

Bales and Shannon take this as a good sign. Talking about money would make the core issue easier to dispense with. "A little bit of sugar ..." is essentially what both are thinking.

But not quite yet.

"We wanted to clear the path first, Marcus, to clarify where we stand," Bales says to deflect getting into specifics. "I'm sure they'll be more than fair, more than fair. There aren't many opportunities like this and they seem to have eager customers in their pocket. The potential is quite large, quite large. We'd be wise to work with them as closely as we can. Very, very closely."

Epps nods and purses his lips. He understands.

Brevan Shannon pushes his cleared plate forward to lean upon the table and take his turn.

"There's more than what they'd pay us – the city, I mean. Sure, the extra money for the budget will be welcome. There are plenty of needs we haven't been able to address for years now. The voters would appreciate seeing those get done. But Putter promised, also, that they'd hire local for this. We need that. It's never gone down well when they'd bus in people from Texas, or wherever, for the cutting and hauling. Then there's that one more big windstorm and we could lose some of those trees anyway. Look what happened during tornado season down south of here. If we had a storm anything like that, it'd be salvage instead of harvest. We'd be beholden to them. We – the city, I mean – would get nothing."

"Shannon's right, Marcus. It would be wise to get value while we can, while Putter and his people have an interest and we have something to offer."

"Well ... those oaks are protected by the City Charter. You know that." Epps lifts his chin to serially turn his face toward his table mates. "If ..."

"We could pass a waiver, Marcus," Bales makes use of the pause to suggest. "Make it a special case situation."

"Possibly," Epps says after another thoughtful pause.

"Not too special," inserts Brevan Shannon, "just as something that needs to be done. Think what would happen if, say, a weakened limb broke off one of those old oaks and came down on kids riding their bikes, or on some poor family having a picnic," he proposes, thinking of the scene he had recently watched. "That would be awful for the city. We'd be held liable. The legal eagles would pounce on that."

"Possibly," Epps, having gone to law school himself, agrees half-heartedly. "But besides the direct protection of the trees, there's the matter of the squirrels."

"What matter?" Bales asks, obviously surprised.

"It's their habitat. They make nests in those old oaks. They're what make the park so pleasant for people."

"Are you kidding me?" Shannon is similarly bewildered. "The squirrels? They're rodents, bushy tailed rats."

"Not everyone thinks so," Epps counters.

"Not everyone pays attention to what damage they do," Shannon says in a slightly louder tone. "They're vermin. Just the other day I –"

**** CHAPTER 4 ****

"We don't need to get the squirrels into this, surely," states Mayor Bales, with a light chuckle, to cut Shannon off. "There are plenty of trees in the woods for them. Plenty of trees. No need to bring them into this. It'll just complicate things. They can easily go somewhere else."

"Or to hell," Brevan Shannon adds resolutely. "Too damn many as it is."

Mayor Bales wants to keep on track. Squirrels aren't his focus. Fewer or none makes no difference to him. He doesn't want them to become an issue standing in the way of getting a lucrative contract signed with Putter. He doesn't have many years left to make his own nest and isn't inclined to be concerned about where they make theirs.

"So, will you be able to draft an exception that they'll go for?"

"An exception?... For taking down, harvesting, as you say, a few of the older big oaks?"

"Exactly, Marcus. But let's not say 'a few.' Say 'some.' No need to be overly specific. That only makes for argument." Bales knows that the opposite is true. Specificity is what avoids debate. But he would prefer post hoc discussion, usually impotent, over a priori limitations. "Let's go over a draft the next day or so. I don't think we should chance losing this opportunity. It could be how we get that wonderful, wonderful senior center extension you've been talking about."

*** *CHAPTER 4* ***

Hayes Bales is a good salesman. He knows he's planted the seed and watered it enough. It's time to let it take root and grow.

Bales inquires about Councilman Epps' family, none of whom he's actually met, and raises several other points of seemingly mutual interest. Their innocuous conversation winding down, they finish their lunch and order coffee. Soon, Marcus taps the table before rising and states that he has errands to run.

"The next day or so, then?" Bales suggests to Epps before he leaves. "You'll call me?"

"Yes. I'll draft something tonight," Epps says in rising.

"Excellent. Excellent," Bales replies as he and Shannon stand to shake hands.

Brevan Shannon and Mayor Bales watch him leave then linger over their coffees, allowing them to be reheated.

"I don't trust that Epps," Shannon says.

"Why's that, Brevan?"

"He always seems to be frowning. Always has that crease between his eyes."

"It's the face he was born with, I'm afraid. That and his almost annoying way of speaking are just the way he is, not a reaction." Bales sniffs and smiles. "Once you understand that, you can use it. He's a team player. He'll get it done for us, I'm very, very sure of that. He knows he has a lot to gain as well. You saw the way he perked up when I mentioned the senior center? That will get him pulling for us, I'm sure. Very sure.

He won't be a councilman forever and he knows it. We need to nudge him along to get a long-term, blanket deal through and not have to deal with season by season renegotiations." He lowers his voice and motions Brevan closer. "Let him take the lead. It'd be better, very much better for everyone. We're not going to be here forever. For some people, people like Epps, very small rewards work better than big, especially when you get near the end. They're less problematic. If a senior center gets a rise out of him, fine, fine. Good ideas need good reasons and beneficial ideas are always good. I think we've given him enough, more than enough."

"Maybe. But I doubt this'll be easy to get done," Shannon admits after a few more slow sips of his coffee. "If we alter the preservation rules –"

"The 'Old Oaks' code?"

"Right. If we try to modify city code we're going to have a big fight on our hands. We'd better duck that, stay outside of that, if you see what I mean." Shannon leans forward. "What we need is a solid reason why some of those oaks absolutely *need* to come down. Maybe all of them. A reason that doesn't involve changing code."

"And that would be?" Bales is eager to know, since Shannon seems to have one in mind.

"Squirrels. The damn squirrels. They're a nuisance and potentially dangerous. That has to be the key issue – making the park safe. They live in those big oaks."

"They live in trees everywhere, Brevan."

"Sure, I realize that. But it's the park we're talking about. Right? So we should make that the point issue. Make the case that the very old oaks harbor the damn squirrels and if we take some of them down, the vermin'll run off, go elsewhere. See? We can throw in that the really old trees have structural issues and present more of a risk now, liability." Shannon leans back in his chair. "It'll sail through. But focus on the pesky squirrels. Fewer oaks, fewer squirrels, so we need to thin out the old oaks. See? No change to old city code. No new code. Just maintenance. Just normal prudent care and preservation to make Oak Park a safe place to have a picnic or walk your damn dog. Problem solved."

Bales reviews what he cautioned Epps just a few moments ago and realizes that altering his view, his stated view at least, makes good sense.

"You're on to something there, my clever, clever friend. Never attack a problem head on. Never head on. It's expected. Find a seam, and go at it from the side, so what you're doing doesn't look like what you're doing! Good man," he chortles. "Good man. It may not be the final answer but it's a good start for us. We can build on it. We'll get the paper to pick up on the squirrel issue, too. You think you can find some people who can speak to that, provide support for it?" Bales grins back at Shannon's affirmative nods. "Good. Good. I'll call Epps as soon as I get back to the office."

CHAPTER FIVE

Mayor Bales stands before the mirror in the little room off his office and cants his head side to side. His over-coifed visage meets with his approval, but still he wonders: Does this suit look sufficiently official, mayoral or better? He can't do anything about his bulk. It comes from years of living large and exercising little. But he can hide it, which, as always, he's careful to do with the aid of well-tailored clothes.

His large head, large hair, and large body ridicule his small hands and feet. The general impression is somewhat like what results from a stone sculptor having overdone a core likeness only to find her/himself with insufficient material for finalizing the peripheral details.

A sports jacket would have sufficed. The council sessions are relatively informal. Few on the council and none in the audience will be as nattily attired as is he. They, however, aren't as needful of casting the proper impression as is Mayor Bales.

It's been a good ride, he thinks to himself, moving from real estate to public service and finding ways to make the latter serve the former. Being Mayor is a chore in some ways, because of the constant visibility and critique. He's been too immersed in both these last few years. Nevertheless, it has not been dull and he has no doubts that he's the best mayor Oakville has ever had, the undoubted and absolute best. His predecessors had done so little and the bulk of that was wrong-headed.

Perfectly consistent with respect to having ambitious aides intent upon ensuring his intentions were realized, prior manipulations have escaped official scrutiny far more than have those more current. The closer he comes to his end, the less significant the former seem to be. Resurrected when he leaves office or not, they soon will have little standing and no practical relevance for him.

Bales has often complained that those he serves and those who serve with him accept his transgressions primarily because of the benefits they receive. He knows how tenuous such love can be. His abiding wish has been to be loved and to have the means, physical as well as financial, to enjoy his whims. Having controlled the means and now gazing upon the reality of his waning years, he strains to have his deeds met with public accolades whether large, small, or misdirected – the accolades as well as the deeds. Say it with a smile and certainty, he thinks to himself as he scans his reflection. Neither tolerating nor bending to the critics – that's the key to mobilizing support. He's the respected mayor of a city with a long history. He has risen to a level beyond his dreams, to a level that, while not definitively establishing his incompetence, has brought him perilously close. Yet, he and his friends have benefitted greatly while doing so. He doesn't want to lose the status he has attained. And, above all, he wants his assets to remain secure and sufficient.

He smiles into the mirror. Through the open door behind he sees Marcus Epps standing by his desk.

"I didn't hear you knock," Bales calls out.

"I didn't."

"Nice crowd? Big crowd?" Bales calls out to his close, close ally on the Oakville City Council.

Most city council meetings are tedious affairs, with repetitious business to readdress, repetitious complaints and pleadings to rehear, repetitious promises and referrals to redirect. Epps earlier had stood at the rear of the Oakville Council room to gauge the tenor of today's crowd. There were enough council members present, he determined, to make a quorum. Plus, there were a sufficient number of recognizable faces to help achieve the goals of the session. Finally, there was the absence of the independent critics, those who often projected impatience with status quo and/or expediency.

"Yes, a fine, supportive crowd, Hays. It's under control, I believe."

*** *CHAPTER 5* ***

"Everyone there as planned?" Mayor Bales asks as he steps back into the office. He wants to be reassured. He doesn't like disappointment and he doesn't like surprises.

"Yes. Brevan indicated that.... I think it's agenda item eight or nine," Epps then ventures.

Bales pokes at the single sheet on his desk, lifts it, then comes back around to stand close to Epps.

"Nine, actually. The last one." Bales looks at his outsized, meant-to-be-impressive gold watch. "Let's go on in."

It's a short walk to the meeting. In larger, wealthier urban areas, city business is dealt with in impressive rooms, with auditorium seating for the audience and an imposing, usually curved table set upon a dais for council members. The eight or ten or twelve elected officials get to sit in comfortable judge's chairs throughout the several hours of a session. Oakville never attained that level of sophistication. Its City Council Room is large but non-specific. It's a general purpose space, with folding chairs – not the sharp-backed cheap metals ones, at least, but chairs with decent padding – set in neat rows. Seven armchairs – six for the council plus one for the Mayor – are arrayed behind a rectangular table. A microphone, printed agenda, and tablet of ruled sheets sit in front of each chair. To the council members' right, a simple, well-worn lectern is provided for those who wish to address them.

As Bales and council members take their seats, a few more folks drift in and scatter themselves amongst the available empty chairs facing them. The attendance, Bales notes, is larger than usual. That's bad, in the sense that today's might be a longer session than usual, but good in the sense that agenda item nine will be showered with the support he has requested. Objections are highly unlikely given that, while published three days ahead as required by city statute, the agenda is seldom familiar to anyone other than the one or several who composed it.

Tapping the table with a distressed gavel, Bales opens this mid-morning's meeting of the Oakville City Council. A number of items of business are taken up then dispensed with after citizens provide their thoughts – limited to three minutes – from the lectern. After presentations by staff and, again, various expressions of opinion from the audience, items three, four, and five each require a vote, which is unanimous and quick. Items six through eight are basically informational and duly noted by the Council Secretary, who sits at a separate table on the left side of the room. One older gentleman rises to state his negative opinion of the need for the study whose progress was explained in item seven. While ill-timed and irrelevant, the complaint is duly noted.

"Agenda item nine," the secretary intones. "Squirrel overabundance in Oak Park."

Several people are at the lectern by the time she has come to the end of the introductory.

"Therefore," she concludes, "the City is to take steps to determine the best manner for relocating, reducing, or removing the population of tree squirrels that have taken residence in the oaks of Oak Park. The common gray squirrel, known by the scientific name of ..." she pauses to pronounce it carefully, "Sciurus carolinensis, is not considered to be an endangered species."

Brevan Shannon, sitting next to his skinny, sour friend, George Martino, tilts toward the woman on his other side and has a few words. She grasps the page of notes on her lap then gets up to join the short queue waiting to speak.

Mayor Bales acknowledges Marcus Epps, who pulls his microphone closer.

"It has come to," he starts, pausing ever so slightly, "to our attention ... the attention of City Council staff ... that the excessive number of squirrels in the trees of Oak Park has become an issue ... perhaps a public health and safety issue. It's the purpose of agenda item nine to establish a plan ... and assign such city and outside personnel as are necessary to carry it out ... for reducing the number of squirrels in the park. Nothing has been set in motion, thus far.... We do need, however, the City Council does seek citizen input as to the reasons for and best manner for carrying this out."

Epps glances into the audience at Brevan Shannon, who looks over to the people lined up to comment then gives a slight nod back to him. Epps proceeds with more confidence.

"The complaints received have ranged from specifics, like disturbing picnickers and frightening small children, to implications of potential issues, like the diseases they may carry and their rodent-like behavior elsewhere than in Oak Park itself.... As they are undomesticated creatures, we cannot train them. Nor can we expect to get rid of them altogether. We can, however, reduce their population and exert some measure of control over their overall behavior and where they have proliferated."

Formally stated, suitably to the point yet not totally anticipatory, Epps' comments receive nods of approval from most at the table, most vigorously from the Mayor.

Dwight Eisen, the Councilman seated two removed from Mayor Bales, speaks up.

"I'd like a moment, Mister Mayor."

"You have the floor," Bales grants him.

"Aren't we being premature in proposing to act against the squirrels in some manner? I've seen the staff's report. Their summary is suggestive but not so definitive as to the need to take action at this time. It would seem to me that –"

"What we need to do, then Mister Eisen, if I may interrupt, is to hear from the citizens who wish to address exactly this issue." Bales then indicates those standing in line. "Would you agree that would be a good way to proceed?"

Eisen has made the comment he planned. He has marked his territory, so to speak, made a show of independence, and is content to wait out the next twenty or thirty minutes of anecdotal testimony.

"I agree, Mister Mayor. Let's hear what the good people, who have taken the time to come before us today, have to say," Eisen graciously concedes.

As each speaker approaches the lectern, some placing a few pages of notes down upon it, they are reminded to give their full name and place of residence. "For the record," the City Secretary repeatedly informs them. In virtually every instance, the speaker either moves in too close to the microphone or positions him/herself too far away. They have to be prompted to adjust.

It's a litany of personal experiences and opinion, some common and predictable in view of the topic, some strange and, even to a biased observer, strained and possibly disingenuous. There are stories of squirrels eating through siding and eaves, and of getting into residential attics where they snack on the wiring.

"Could've caused a fire if the breaker hadn't tripped," that speaker adds.

A few heads in the audience nod sympathetically. Those behind the table remain passively attentive and noncommittal as the citizens proceed. Tales of garbage cans being ransacked, of dogs being teased, of the potential for unknown diseases and indubitable fleas being spread are told and elaborated upon as each speaker's time allows. Complaints of chewed house and car wires, of gnawed woodwork and decor, of consumed landscaping are offered again and again. Another tells, in humorous detail as if rehearsed, of the damage done by a squirrel – female, he has no doubt – that took up residence under his pickup's hood, against the firewall.

"Ate through the wires to the AC compressor, so it stopped working. Ate through the thick insulation of one of the damn AC lines, too. Excuse me, but I had to replace everything and it wasn't cheap, for sure."

Despite having been advised of their time restriction, the supportive speakers' allocations typically expire in mid-sentence. Virtually each has to be cautioned to conclude. None is perturbed, however. What they had planned to say they said.

"And then my dog chased the squirrel. Almost got it," one gentlewoman testifies. "Now, what if she had caught the thing and it had rabies? That would've been terrible."

"Well, who the hell's fault would that be, then," comes in a tired voice from some uncertain spot in the audience.

Mayor Bales bangs the gavel. "Please," he says. "None of that. Finish your remarks, please, ma'am."

As she does so, which comprises just a few short sentences of repetition, Brevan Shannon leans to his right.

"'The squirrel chased your dog,' in the park, I told her," he says very softly to his friend, Martino, with a shake of his head. "*It* chased *your* dog," he repeats, spreading his fingers wide upon his knees.

Martino silently mimics the gesture and adds gentle pats upon his baggy pant legs.

"None of it's really new. Doesn't make any difference," Shannon then chooses to observe. "Just have to get it out in a bunch."

Finally, the last of the speakers having told of scattered detritus in the park, interrupted lunch breaks, and disturbed picnics ("Worse than ants, believe you me.") Mayor Bales hikes himself forward and keys on his microphone. It's not needed in the smallish space, but it makes his voice, hence his presence, seem even larger.

"It seems that there's considerable evidence to suggest that we must do something about the squirrels in Oak Park, perhaps about squirrels in general," he says.

"Just get rid of them," suggests Brevan Shannon, loud enough to be heard but not to draw undo attention to himself.

"Right. It's our park, not the damn squirrels'," comes loudly from someone nearby. A ripple of assent flows over the audience, a spreading disruption, much like when a pebble is tossed into a pond, and similarly instigated. Shannon looks down at his hands and smiles.

"There are several possibilities," Bales continues, without acknowledging this break in decorum. "We could try to scare them off with predator calls and decoys. I've tried that around my house, I'll confess, and it didn't do much good. Guard dogs might work, but that doesn't seem very practical. The park shouldn't be like a prison, I would point out. Then there are humane traps. We could capture and relocate them but, personally, I'm afraid they'd just return, especially when there's a good crop of acorns. They seem to be attracted to the large acorns from those old trees. I'd hate to think about poisoning them, but that also is an option. I –"

"May I interrupt here, Mister Mayor?"

Dwight Eisen has made a point of showing rapt attention throughout the proceedings and feels this is the point to offer another opposing view. He glances at Epps, sitting not far from him at the council table, before continuing.

"I concede that there *may* be a problem. I'm not convinced that there is but many others seem to be, so I won't categorically object. I do, however, think we need to think carefully about this. *Some* squirrels can be annoying, even harmful at *some* times. That doesn't mean we need to take drastic action. Poisoning them certainly would be excessive in my view. Just think of the consequences. I –"

"Which would be?" Marcus Epps asks.

"Well," Eisen leans forward and turns slightly to reply, "firstly, if they were to consume the poison and left to die somewhere, wouldn't that cause issues of its own? Other animals could consume them, even the occasional pet, I suppose, if off leash, and could get sick. Also and more basic, I believe, is that we haven't yet considered what good, what benefits we derive from the squirrels. They're generally harmless. They're fun for the children to watch and feed when they come to the park. The acorns that they store away eventually yield new oaks, especially in the surrounding forests. We might, in fact, simply consider limiting them to the forest," he puts forward. "They don't have to be a constant presence in Oak Park."

"Well, I'm not sure how we could do that. Limit where the squirrels live, I mean," Epps notes. "They won't simply do what we say, Dwight, even were we to pass an ordinance."

Many in the audience and even several facing it laugh at this last assertion. "Can squirrels read?" is heard to float out over the discussion. "Ticket a squirrel???" chuckles another attendee.

Although he detects he's the focus of the laughter, Eisen persists.

"I'm simply trying to point out that the squirrels provide a degree of benefit and we should not focus solely on the problems they may or may not be causing."

"Are causing, Mister Eisen," the Mayor says. "We're attempting to address the problems they *are* causing."

"We need to consider what would be the implications of dispersing the squirrels, removing them from Oak Park. We can't deal with this using anecdotes and fears, which may be more imagined than real. We need to use reason."

"You're always saying that, Dwight," Councilman Epps tells him.

"Well, what's wrong with reason and making use of facts? We, ourselves sometime cause problems. We have our own flaws," Eisen says, in a tone that suggests he's nearly finished with his comments.

"Th'hell we do," comes from the audience.

*** *CHAPTER 5* ***

Mayor Bales taps the table gently with his gavel.

"We should not blow a small problem up into a big one," Eisen adds before leaning back in his chair.

But this is precisely Bales' aim.

Council meetings in general, in big cities as well as small, can go on like this for hours, with small bubbles of personal concerns inflated into profound truths and, the points raised often being multiform and conflicting, ending up in endless debate. The Oakville City Council meeting is adjourned with little formally resolved. The squirrel issue, however, has been inserted into the public record. One additional step, indeed the primary goal, was also achieved. With careful management Mayor Bales succeeded in getting authorization to have an expert advise them as to the best course of action. He and Epps knew precisely what Dwight Eisen would propose, namely, the need for facts and careful consideration. They only had to wait for him to say it.

There have been no accusations, no threats, no hints of actionable events for which the city might be responsible. Yet, having the potential dangers made clear, Oakville would have no excuse were a child to be bitten, were a pet to be given rabies or fleas. They have been put on notice, much as if someone had pointed out a tree limb and warned: "That's going to fall, you know, in the next big wind." The palpability of risk and its associated potential liability has been enhanced. Epps and Eisen, in the foreground, with the preparative support from Shannon, Martino, and their contacts at the newspaper in the background, have done their jobs well.

In sum, having formalized the idea that the squirrels needed to be dealt with, the next step will be to define how and thus get to the core of their plan. As Shannon and the Major had mapped out, the squirrels will be deemed prevalent in Oak Park precisely because of the large oaks they favor. If their behavior cannot be controlled directly by altering what they do, then it will have to be modified indirectly, by removing the attraction, that is, by altering what they *want* to do.

Converting that logical sequence into a plan of action will be relatively easy, given the right expert. Outside consultants serve best when they know their fees have been approved and what they have to do to justify them. Both had been taken care of even before the Council met.

* * * * *

Sitting across the desk from Mayor Bales, Brevan Shannon is relaxed and effusive.

"That went well, I'd have to say."

"Yes, it did, Shannon. Very, very well."

"The consultant's report is nearly finished. I had him start on it right after we met with Epps. I'll make sure they have copies by the end of the week. It'll roll along nicely after that." Shannon smiles. He knows he's earned his keep, at least for now.

"Does it have options for them to consider? That might take a long, long time. Maybe even another open meeting." Mayor Bales is not frowning, but it's clear he'd prefer that everything, *everything* be under control.

"No options, Hayes. It's a very clear and direct report with only one viable option. Want to see it?" Shannon leans to one side, where he has set his battered brown leather briefcase.

"Just tell me the bottom line."

"We're going to run with making it so they, the damn squirrels, should have no reason to be in Oak Park." He raises his eyebrows. "What it says is that the big oaks there have to go. He proposes that when he takes into account their age and weakened state – the possibility of a windstorm knocking one over or even just snapping limbs – plus the way in which the squirrels rely on them and the problems that they in turn are causing, the best idea is to reduce the vermin's habitat, to take out some and – Wait," Shannon interjects when Bales starts to protest. "Wait. I know what you're worried about and that's taken care of. 'Some' is his first step. To really solve the problem, not just lessen it, he proposes that *all* those big oaks, the ones called the Founders Oaks, need to be removed from the park. That's going to be his summary finding. He just thinks, and I agree, that it's better to ease into it. You know, sort of the 'cooking the frog' idea."

"But soon? Very, very soon?" Bales asks in a flurry.

"Putter's crews should be able to start before the end of the month," Shannon is pleased to be able to report. "Before Thanksgiving for sure. Winter's a good time for logging. No leaves. By spring no one'll care, believe me. The good folks out there," Shannon waves toward the window, "think about what is, not what was, and not very much about what will be, if handled right. Give them something to be afraid of or hate and the rest is easy."

Neither entertains visions of sugar plums. The prospect, however, of a substantial Christmas "bonus" warms both their hearts.

"That's excellent, Shannon, excellent." Bales nods several times. "I'll sit down with Putter and get the details worked out. We've done our part and it's up to him to do his, if you see what I mean." He folds his arms across his chest. "One question," he smiles at his aide. "Where did you find those people to come down here and speak?"

Brevan leans over his briefcase again, this time taking out a packet of coupons, which he tosses onto the big desk.

"What're these?" Bales asks.

"Coupons for free Sedici! Sixteen ounce coffees." Shannon takes advantage of the Mayor's examination to add, "You'd be surprised how well that works. Small rewards. Right? Plus, a couple of them wanted me, us, to work on getting dogs allowed on restaurant patios. I told them you'd be happy to."

"Certainly. Anything for loyal voters. Anything."

"Later," Shannon clarifies, "after this gets done, I told them."

"Certainly, certainly."

* * * * *

The next week, following a brief City Council session, which could be held in camera because the singular "Squirrel Overabundance" issue had been inserted into a consent agenda, Mayor Bales and his aide, Brevan Shannon, meet after lunch to review the progress of their project. Everything is proceeding as planned, it appears. Marcus Epps is scheduled to join them.

"Why didn't you have the three of us go to lunch?" Shannon asks after a few moments of generalities.

"Epps? I find him difficult, very difficult to take for very long. I never know if he's going to say what I expect or even if he's going to say anything at all. Doesn't he remind you of one of those turtles we'd see poking their necks out of the water down in the creek?"

"That's something I haven't thought about in years, sneaking a joint down by the creek," Shannon says with a grin. "But, sure, he does look that way sometimes."

"He does. And I'd much, much prefer to talk with him here, where we can focus. We needed a solution, so he helped us create the problem that made the solution we wanted a necessity. He's useful, but he's not someone I enjoy socializing with," Bales admits breezily. "We won't have to chit-chat as much here as we would've at lunch."

"Good way to proceed: Solution first, problem second."

Brevan Shannon then allows a broad smile. Hays is not disinclined to chit-chat, he well knows. He does, however, prefer it to be his chit-chat, for it to be his topic and for him to be at the center of it. A brief buzz from the intercom on his desk is the prelude to Sylvia informing him that "Councilman Epps" has arrived.

"Tell him to come right on in," Bales says loudly. He wants everyone in the reception area to hear his friendly dominance. He swivels his chair slightly but remains seated as he motions for Epps to take a seat next to Brevan.

"Greetings, Marcus," the latter offers.

"Yes, hello," replies Epps to him and then, with a longer glance, to Bales.

"Was there much discussion, Marcus?" the Mayor wants to determine.

"No ... Not really. Eisen had a few words but nothing substantial. He thought trapping any squirrels that caused trouble and relocating them would be the better way to go. But ... So we pointed out how slow that would be, how long it would be before we saw ... before there were any tangible results. And, more to the point, we explained the consultant's view that they'd just return once let loose, wherever that was. There would be no end to it."

He lifts his poor excuse for a chin and pushes it forward slightly.

"Yes, yes, Marcus, exactly," Bales says. "Terribly, terribly slow. And not definitive." He does his best not to look at Shannon. "Not every squirrel's objectionable, but we have to treat them all as if they are. The quicker the better. With less reason to be in the park, fewer will. Fewer will want to be."

"It didn't come to much, but Eisen had many reasons to wait, as usual.... He's not one for action," Epps reports, stretching his chin farther forward. "It's done, though. We've got the authorization you wanted." He pats his jacket. "It was a good idea to have that small ... that small hint of reluctance. It makes everything else seem ... seem proper."

"Well, you can reason yourself into anything, if you have a mind to," Bales tells him. "I prefer to trust my gut, my instinct, and just get on with what needs to be done," he quickly adds.

"That's what animals do," Epps observes and immediately wishes he hadn't.

A small smile invades Shannon's features.

"Are you saying we're more like the squirrels than we realize? Maybe they should get together and kick *us* the hell out of *their* park."

*** *CHAPTER 5* ***

It's Shannon's jocular aside, but one not appreciated by Bales any more than was Epps' original observation. Through his shallow but steady rise, he had never appreciated being put on the defensive and often blunted any such attempt by being the aggressor. In this instance it's too early in the process for that. He needs Epps and doesn't want to antagonize him. Relaxing back, forcing his mind to dismiss the private zoomorphic overlay on Epps that has taken form, he goes along with his aide's deflection.

"Well, we're bigger and we're smarter. Much smarter. So we'll be in charge. Marcus, I'm very, very glad that we're going to be able to get that contract signed with the lumbermen. It's an excellent, excellent solution. It'll mean a lot of good, good things for Oakville. Like that senior center. I'm sure some squirrels would be fine, if they stayed in the park, I mean. But, then, which?"

If he were to express his mind forthrightly, Mayor Bales would not be inclined to say a good word about any squirrel. To have them be gone is both a fictive problem solved and a means for ensuring that a real opportunity has been solidified. It never occurs to him – it never will – that the small benefit he and his cohorts shall receive is paltry compared to the sense of loss that many will come to feel.

CHAPTER SIX

All is proceeding as Mayor Bales, Brevan Shannon, and the good folks from Putter Hardwoods – the company's new appellation – planned. Epps, in his quiet, seemingly objective but personally rewarding manner, was able to guide the City Council from idea to implementation over a surprisingly short time span. Those in need of street repairs or more police presence in their neighborhoods, the parents hoping to have the public library receive the new study carrels that were promised but never budgeted, the community activists clamoring for more shelter space for the homeless, who are in relatively small numbers in Oakville but physically stressed in the winter, and the many others who wished to receive more attention from the city would have been delighted to have their concerns dealt with one half, one quarter, one tenth the diligence.

*** *CHAPTER 6* ***

Many of the large oaks in Oak Park are gone, their former places marked by stumps that eventually will be ground away. The largest are thereby most noticeable by their absence but, it being December and too cold for spending time in the park, no meaningful opposition has arisen. In fact, since Shannon Brevan made sure the local paper did a detailed piece – a followup actually – on the new road maintenance equipment that the enhanced lumber contract has enabled it to contract for, there's been an undercurrent of approval. Nothing overt, mind you, but enough orchestrated acceptance to preclude embarrassing confrontations. Come spring, there will be virtually no oaks in Oak Park to harbor the pesky squirrels that were the proximate rationale of the plan to remove them. Of course not.

Desire is the fuel that enables effort. Need, whether real or imagined, is the origin of desire. Therefore, it will be important going forward that the people of Oakville feel no need to reverse the action that is underway. The Mayor and his cohorts have received the means to satisfy many of their desires. These rewards were enhanced by making the arrangements for the benefit of Putter's company fixed and long-standing. The amount of heartwood that it's been able to acquire is more than they had anticipated, a most welcome turn of events for which they've been most appreciative.

There must be no thoughts of a reversal now that the program is underway. It didn't take much time to remove Founders Oaks that had stood tall for so many generations.

*** *CHAPTER 6* ***

Everything possible must be done to ensure that the agreements made won't be abrogated or altered. Since such pressures often come from those who haven't experienced direct benefit, there must be great pains taken to keep such malcontents otherwise engaged. And as for the young – those who don't take the benefits awarded to others as sufficient to condition their own action – as well as those receiving the benefits of education – those who often are prone to challenge the prevailing order because that's what maturing, thoughtful youths do – they must be dissuaded, their contrary desires must be precluded.

* * * * *

The design of the low iron fence that surrounds the Oakville Public Library is old fashioned, as is the building itself. Myriad layers of protective paint have softened sharp edges, given the fence character, some would say. Nathan rubs his hand lightly over it as he walks to the concrete entry path. Serious and studious, he regularly goes to the library after school. In addition to picking out one of the assigned books to take home, he often will simply browse the stacks, particularly the history section, the area of study of which he is most fond. While not overly sensitive to the cold, Nathan has been entertaining thoughts of a warm spring and a park to play in. These will be made more tangible if he has the proper book to read over the upcoming Christmas break. In parallel, he's been thinking about what his father told him about Oakville's park and the city's origins.

Nathan doesn't like that Mrs. Black has been replaced. The heavy glasses hanging from a frog around her neck, her wrinkled and pinched face, the faint odor that Nathan could not name but identified as "old" were virtually the exact opposite of the well-dressed, fragrant, and, even at his barely pubescent stage, undeniably pretty Miss White who has taken her place. But the former's warm acceptance of his inquisitive ignorance had made her so approachable. She would listen to his request, walk him to the ancient card file, then, after a moment or two of rummaging, hand him a card and point, with the eraser end of her ever present pencil, at the locator number.

"Bring the card back with you when you check out," she would instruct him, as if he needed that reminder after so many similar helpful searches. At first, he had vaguely wondered how she knew where to put the card back. By the time he entered middle school, he knew. He became adept at using the card file himself, even though at first a few of the topmost drawers were a trifle out of his reach and he needed the aid of a step stool. Now in the seventh grade, he needs Mrs. Black less and the step stool not at all, but he misses her more.

No one removes cards from the card file any longer. Indeed, Oakville's small and underfunded library is still one of the few that uses the printed 3 by 5 cards. Nathan has his note pad out and a pencil ready to mark down a brief version of the title and the full locator number of the book he's after. He can't remember the exact title, but it's the one that describes the very early history of Oakville and tells of the people who came from Europe with their ideas and their ambition. It's the one that reifies those who created the city of Oakville, those who planted the carefully boxed young shoots that would become the Founders Oaks, as Father has told. He has witnessed their recent demise and wonders why, after apparently such a long time, it's become necessary to remove them. In addition to their history being interesting in itself, Nathan intends to use it – or them, if he can find several similar works – as the basis for the theme paper he must turn in by the end of next term.

Unable to remember enough of the full title to extract its location from the card file, Nathan uses the expedient of noting that most of the titles in the subject section he has isolated have similar locator numbers. He will, he decides, go to that area of the stacks and browse. Whether by luck or by jogging his recollection, he should be able to find what he's looking for, the book his father has often mentioned recently.

Alone in a musty aisle, he's glad to have grown sufficiently tall to access the books on the top shelf. A ladder is close by, should he need it. Several bound volumes are peeking over the edge, but "Never pull on the spine," he recalls Mrs. Black having admonished him. Scanning their titles is enough to reveal those are too general, dealing with the state, the country, and the world. He's searching for that which deals specifically with local history. At last, in the next bay, he finds a shelf with suitably suggestive titles. There are less than a dozen, so he makes a heavy, wobbly stack of them and goes to a table by the window. Most appear new, with bright jackets. Only a few show the wear that would suggest they've been on the shelf for some time, that they've been perused by many.

Several focus on Chamber of Commerce "What and Where" types of information. He glances at these, noting that Oak Park is only mentioned without elaboration. Finding no useful accompanying pictures, he pushes them to one side. *Oakville's Bicentenary* is written in gilt on the spine of a large format book. He's never seen or heard the title's second word. It's not difficult for him to puzzle out, however – *bi*, which means two, and *centenary*, which suggests something to do with a hundred years. Two hundred years. Feeling sure it pertains to the appropriate period, he places it as the first of a separate stack. He adds to that *A Brief History of Oakville,* which is a thin paperback he hopes will not belie its title.

Growing Up in the Woods seems an apt selection, because the surrounding forest – a haphazard collection of oaks, maples and chestnuts, with creeks and paths to explore – has yielded him and his friends many adventures. Nathan considers himself someone who could, at some later date, stake a similar claim and perhaps write a similar book. He has much to learn first, as he well knows. He glances at its table of contents then flips through its pages. It's an autobiography of sorts and not really history, he thinks to himself. Nevertheless reading a few paragraphs near the middle, he notes that it's written in a very casual, folksy voice. The selected section is one wherein the author writes of maneuvering a fallen log across Oak Creek, deep in the woods in the early spring, when it was bank to bank with snowmelt and over a foot deep, almost a river.

It might make for an interesting read and suggest new adventures, Nathan considers. He hasn't finished growing up, he thinks. He'll be in Oakville for at least another five years. This summer he and his friends could perhaps build a proper bridge at that same spot, using thin logs, branches, and binder twine, like they show in the scout manual. It would be fun then to see if it lasts through a winter or two. In growing older and feeling the changes this is bringing about, he's becoming more attune to longevity and what it means, as well as to history.

Nathan places the book with the latter, selected stack, but it isn't precisely what he's looking for now.

The other books he scans are remarkable in providing little detail about the Oakville pioneers other than where they came from and when. Nathan is specifically interested in learning about their early life here, about how they came to bring the oak tree shoots and why they planted them here, as his father had told him on more than one visit to Oak Park. He finds brief descriptions of the latter but no mention of the ancient and therefore huge oak trees that he remembers, which he knows because he'd been told, were called the Founders Oaks. His smooth brow wrinkles in that same fashion as when Mother reminds him of something he has promised to do but has not. It reflects puzzlement, certainly, but also the annoyance and tentative denial only recently suitable to his years.

As taught to do, he leaves the rejected volumes for the library staff to shelve. He sets the *Growing Up* ... and other two volumes on the edge of the reference desk.

"Miss White?" he starts.

She takes off her stylish glasses and looks up from rereading the memo she's just finished composing.

"Yes, Nathan?"

"I was trying to find a book but can't."

"What book is that?"

"I'm not sure exactly, but it's the one about those huge trees in the park. It called *The History of the Founders Oaks*, I think, or something like that."

"Founders Oaks? Hmmm. I don't recall that, but I'll check." Miss White swivels toward her computer and types. "We've kept the card catalog file but it's not very accurate now.... Hmmm," she hums again as she scans the screen.

"I went to the stacks," Nathan goes on to tell her.

"I see.... Founders Oaks, you said. Well, I don't find anything with that title." She takes the books Nathan has selected. "Did you want to check these out?... Next time you come in I'll have had a chance to find the other one you're looking for, or something similar."

Still smiling as Nathan leaves, Miss White turns back to her computer. Her smile slowly fades. Glancing at Nathan's back, she types, scrolls down, and has the cursor highlight the entry starting "Founders Oaks, Oakville." The title shown is *A History of Founders Oaks*. Its locator number indicates it should be in the Regional History area. An appended note, however, shows the book to be safely locked away in the reference cabinet behind her. She gets up to verify that. Returning to her desk, she places it next to the keyboard. She thinks for a moment before opening her mail client and starting to type.

"Hays," she starts then backspaces to erase that.

"Mayor Bales:" she restarts. "A young man was today asking about that history of Oak Park book you mentioned some time ago." She taps the desk in front of her keyboard with the tips of her shaped nails. "It's put away along with the others, as you wished. But if you don't think it should be accessible, then it shouldn't be here, in the library. I'm not here all the time. Let me know what I should do. And call me, please."

As a matter of habit, she starts to enter her given name but backspaces over that also.

"Ms. White, Library."

For giving her the present of Mrs. Black's job, Mayor Bales has asked little in return, aside from the occasional surreptitious pleasure – which, because of the upstate venue and fine dinner, is reciprocal – and some help with clearing out unwanted volumes from the library. The Mayor, being older, is easy to please and she, being younger, has much time ahead of her. It was time consuming, however, going through the illustrated children's books in the library, as he had requested, and being sure that none remained that lauded big oak trees or playful squirrels. The latter, in particular, required a good bit of culling. Her careful oversight over any potential new acquisition will serve to ensure that this omission, which was really more of a commission, will be sustained. Books about or featuring squirrel-like characters were not forbidden, of course. It was just that such had not to put such creatures in a good light. Bushy tailed creatures, if any, had to be incidental, apart from any main thrust of the story. Even better, any book that had a squirrel as a villain – a biter or scratcher, perhaps, or a carrier of fleas or disease – was eagerly adopted by the acquisition committee that she headed.

"It's okay for a book to include them if they're like the snake in the bible," Bales had hoarsely confided one night as they lay side by side, he tired and spent, she just tired.

* * * * *

During dinner that evening, Nathan shared with his parents his idea of making the topic of his spring theme the

Founders Oaks, how they got there, what they mean, and the possible reasons for them being cut down.

"Good idea," Norman replied. "Do you remember what I told you about them?"

"Only some of it, Dad. I'm getting a book about them from the library. Miss White is helping me."

Norman and Marianne exchange looks.

"She's pretty isn't she?" Nathan's mother asks.

"I guess.... She didn't find it right off. *History of Founders Oaks*. Isn't that what you said the title was?"

"Yes," Norman says slowly, beginning to think more about his son's plan. "Something like that. Already checked out?"

"No. It wasn't there and she didn't see it listed. But she said she'd get it for me."

"I don't like the park anymore," Victoria states.

"Why not, Vicky?" Marianne asks her.

"I don't know. I just don't."

"She's scared of the squirrels," Nathan proposes.

"They'll be pretty much gone next time we go," his father tells the two of them. "No need to fret about them."

"I told you I'd chase them away," Nathan asserts with a hint of manly swagger.

"No, you didn't."

"I did!"

"Stop that. Finish your dinner," their father states firmly

**** CHAPTER 6 ****

Norman purses his lips while he takes a good look at his son. He has a decision to make and feels the need to talk with Marianne before doing so.

After the dinner dishes have been put away, Norman goes to his desk in the corner of their spacious den. He leans back in the leather chair he received as a surprise Father's Day gift. The book that's been on his mind since dinner is in a drawer, not hidden exactly, but where visitors' eyes would not spot it – *A History of Founders Oaks*. He flips over a few pages then goes back and rereads the subtitle: *The Early Settlers of Oakville and What the Oaks Symbolized for Them.* He can still recognize many of the places in the park shown in its illustrations. One large, sepia toned image, obviously among the oldest in the compilation, shows mustachioed men in braces and straw hats looking upon two others who, with linked arms, are barely able to encircle a huge oak. He smiles, imagining that he knows exactly where that tree stands. Or, as he thinks further with a small frown, where it once stood.

"You're still beautiful," he says to his wife out of nowhere when they are getting ready for bed. He has no ulterior motive, just sincere admiration and thanks for the many years they've had together.

"Why, that's very nice of you to say. Only, I'm not sure about that 'still' part." She softens the critique with a smile.

"I have that book Nathan was talking about," he tells her.

"You have it? Really? Here in the house?"

"Sure. I've had it for years. It's where I got those stories to tell the kids, stories about the park. I thought they would like to have it to look through for themselves when they start getting interested in where they've grown up, curious about their past, our past.... If they ever do."

"Oh, they will, Honey. I'm sure. Once they're old enough to start thinking about their own mortality."

"Wow, Sweet. That's good. Classy. 'Their own mortality,'" he repeats. "But I suppose that's exactly right. Most people tend to put things off until another day. They're so sure there always'll be one."

"That's what I meant. The past becomes more important, somehow, when the future starts to have limits."

"I have to say, I thought I was the thinker in the family." Norman says this in a sincere, mildly self-deprecating tone. "I guess I think more with my hands now than my head."

"You do, Honey. And I love when you do."

His face breaks into a broad smile and feels slightly warm. He walks to his only wife, his only partner, and gives her a kiss, a hug, then another, briefer kiss.

"Time for bed," he suggests.

"I think so, too," she smiles back.

"Anyway, I'll give Nathan that book so he can write a good report or theme paper, whatever they call it now."

"I'm not sure you should do that, Norman."

"What? Why?"

"We don't want him to get into trouble. Oak Park is quite different now. Most of those big oaks are gone. They went to a lot of trouble to make sure we didn't make a fuss about that. Made it like they had to do it. So I'm sure they wouldn't want it to be brought up again." Marianne pauses on the way to their bathroom. "Especially, they wouldn't like to have a young person writing a report about it."

Norman sits on the edge of the bed and runs his hand along one edge of the turned down covers.

"I hadn't thought about that," he says. "About his possibly getting into trouble, I mean."

"Well, we should," Marianne calls back

"I'll put it back in the drawer and keep it to myself then," he tells her when she returns. "I'll give it to him when he's older, maybe when he's going off to college. He's got years to grow. It might be better for him to think about things like that when he's old enough to –"

"And wise enough," Marianne returns to insert.

"Yes, old enough and wise enough to realize what it means. Maybe things'll be different, back to how they were."

"Let's hope. Goodnight."

"That's it?" Norman says with a mock pout. "Just 'Goodnight'?"

"Well, how about ... Goodnight, Honey."

They both laugh, switch off their respective table lamps, pull up the covers, then turn to look into each other's eyes.

CHAPTER SEVEN

It's a frosty December morning. The issue uppermost on the squirrels' agenda these past weeks has been gathering and storing away what they'll need for the cold months. The acorn crop is abundant. They're rich with fat and carbohydrates. The squirrels ate some and buried many. From the latter will come seedlings to replace oaks taken by disease, storm, or humans. Some, after sprouting, will serve only as food for browsers. It's wasteful, perhaps, but part of the natural cycle that's persisted for as long as have the squirrels. That will be mainly in the heart of the forest, however. In Oak Park, the steady maintenance, the groomed grassy areas, and the constant visitation by humans provide little opportunity for saplings of any substantial size to develop. On the other hand, since the oaks were protected, there was no need.

*** *CHAPTER 7* ***

Autumn was nothing like those of years past when, for reasons the humans try to explain but the squirrels merely have to experience, the oak mast was scanty, the acorns small, and the seeds within poorly developed. This winter won't find them short of food. The squirrels' concern is focused elsewhere, on the activity they've noticed among the oaks of Oak Park and in the surrounding forest. They had grown accustomed to the latter. It's the annual timber harvest, one perhaps just a bit more active than usual. The former, on the other hand, is unusual. Until now, they've been quite content to be in Oak Park and, in accordance with tradition, always established a goodly number of their nests there.

The morning sun is melting the frost that has settled on the twigs and branches. Small beads of water form lenses that sparkle as the sun climbs higher. Active, after cozy sleep in high perches, many squirrels are moving among the bare limbs, occasionally pausing to shake accumulated moisture from their coats. Twitch, easily recognizable by his outsized eyes and hyperactive tail, looks down at a broad, beige stump, the dust from the chain saw and the gouge in the turf from the hauler still in evidence. Sandy and his mentor, Caesar, arrive and grip the round bulk of a nearby branch.

"There's another one," Twitch says in a tone that suggests complaint.

"Another one what?" Sandy asks.

"Another stump. That means they've taken down another oak. A big one, too. I've seen others."

"Duh," Sandy says uncharitably. "You sure they didn't just plant a stump?"

"Stop badgering him, Sandy," Caesar sighs. Then, to Twitch, he says, "I know. Several of the big oaks have been cut down and taken off. Nothing much we can do about that." Caesar has been mulling over the unexpected cutting but tries not to let his apprehension show.

"And nests went with them," Twitch reports. "I think everyone got away okay, though. There weren't any ... any kits."

"They'll be okay. There's time to build new ones." Sandy observes. "I hope they'll be smart enough to go deep into the forest for that. Where are Cody and Kiki, by the way? Hope they haven't killed each other. They're always at it. Has anyone seen them?"

Caesar and Twitch shake their heads.

"No," the former states. "I suppose they're out there somewhere, chasing each other as usual. There's more to conflict than the fighting. You have to have an aim or it's pointless."

"They'll eventually grow up," Sandy offers as his hopeful opinion. "But ..." He gets the expected looks of agreement.

"Snow's coming," Caesar changes topic to observe. "Soon, and a lot."

"You think?" Sandy replies.

*** *CHAPTER 7* ***

"A lot of snow? Yes, I do. This many acorns must mean a very cold winter is ahead," Caesar explains. There are many reasons why this may be so. He could not articulate any, however, since he has only a limited memory of past winters. What he does have is the experience of several more than the average squirrel. Even more importantly, he has the instinct that's come down through his ancestors.

"Is that a guess or a prediction, Caesar?"

"Does it matter?" the older squirrel replies to Sandy, peering down along the trunk of the oak they occupy, as if to determine if there's any reason to think that it, also, will soon be taken down. "How's the caching?" he then asks him. "Everyone doing their part?"

"It seems so," Sandy replies. "There were deer browsing but there's more than enough mast, even out there, in the forest. Everyone's been busy putting acorns away." He looks back as Jolie scampers down from a nest above.

"Everyone except for Mel, there," she complains.

The object of her disdain has been clinging to the trunk beside his paramour, Mae. He flips sideways and grinds his teeth, clearly unconcerned whether he has or has not contributed fairly to the troupe's winter needs.

"The acorns here are tastier. And bigger, like the oaks they fell from," Sandy adds.

"Bigger *is* better," Mae offers. "Don't you think, Mel?"

Heretofore quietly amusing himself, and some of the squirrels higher in this and nearby trees, by gyrating on the end of a flexible branch, Beater hops back toward its more stable proximal portion.

"There they are. Mel and Mae, sitting in a tree," he chants.

Mel makes a feint in his direction.

"All she needs is love," Beater croons, backing away and trying not to be repetitious. "All she needs is love, love. Love is all she needs."

He and the other squirrels take note when Caesar chatters for them to pay attention.

"I hope you'll all remember," he states to those within earshot, "where you buried what you collected. I can tell it's going to be a severe winter, with lots of ice and snow. We're going to need every bit. And don't plan on storing much here, around these trees."

True or not, accurate or not, his first suggestion is an appropriate cautioning for those who might be tempted to consume rather than save. His second is not totally received by them. They may heed but won't be sure why.

"What's going on with the stumps, like that one?" Mel asks as if to illustrate the latter uncertainty. He turns about to balefully stare down at what remains of the recently harvested huge white oak. "There wasn't any storm. It looks like they cut it down on purpose. And there are more like that over there." His head bobs several times.

"Yes, they didn't just fall over," Sandy sarcastically offers. "They were cut, with those noisy saws. And it's not only here," he further informs them. "A lot of oaks have been taken from the forest, too. Some very big ones, too. More than usual."

"There's more than the stumps that are new," Beryl puts in. "Have you noticed those signs that've gone up? The ones with something that kind of looks like one of us drawn inside a big red circle with a bar across it?"

"I have," says Jolie. "What do they mean?"

"Some of the drawings had more than a squirrel," Sandy contributes. "They showed a human hand holding out a bit of food to a squirrel face. Those had those same red circles and diagonal cross bars. I've seen signs like that before, by the side of the road, and watched cars stop and turn around like they aren't supposed to go any farther. One by the picnic area has a picture of a fire circled and barred, like they aren't supposed to do that either. I don't understand human, but what those signs mean isn't hard to figure out. They're showing what not to do. Just because we can't speak or read human doesn't mean we're stupid, does it?"

"No, it doesn't. And that's part of it, I'm afraid," Caesar sighs. "They're convinced we *are* ignorant. But we're not stupid creatures because we can't communicate with them, any more than they're stupid because they can't communicate with us."

"Too subtle for me," Mel admits.

"I like subtle," he hears in Mae's hoarse whisper.

His only reaction is to give her a long, curious look.

"What I'm getting at," Sandy resumes, "is that the new signs, the ones with drawings of us on them, are telling me that they don't want people to feed us. Take a look at those drawings of us. Who has big teeth sticking out like that? Beavers and rats maybe, not us. I think they're trying to make humans be afraid of us."

"Why the hell make them frightened of us? I could give them a good scare if I had a mind to, but I don't." Mel illustrates his point by wrinkling his nose to bare his incisors then snapping his jaws together. "Never have."

"No," says Twitch, "just us and little girls." He moves a few body lengths farther away in response to Mel's glare.

"Exactly, Mel. That's not what we are. Think about all we do even without being able to communicate with them, the humans. We amuse them, I think it's safe to say. They point and throw snacks, take pictures. Even the young oaks are our doing. Without us there probably wouldn't be new oaks to replace the ones they take or that dry up or get blown over. Besides, the acorns would pile up and make a mess. Why now be making us out to be harmful or threatening? Something's changed, I'd say," Caesar tells him and, by extension, the others within earshot. "Twitch has been in the woods checking on that."

Twitch, made more confident by being singled out, sits upright and flicks his tail. He pulls his forepaws in close.

*** *CHAPTER 7* ***

"They want us out," Caesar says. "They seem to think it'd be better if we weren't here. That's why they're cutting down the oaks. To get rid of us."

"That doesn't make sense," Beryl interrupts. "If they cut down the oaks, then *they* won't have them, whether we're here or not."

"I guess that doesn't matter," Sandy offers as his tenuous opinion. "It's what they *think* will happen that counts."

"How would you know any of that," Mel grumbles. "What do any of you know? You can't read what the signs say or really know why any of it."

"We can see what people are doing," Twitch is bold enough to answer back. "What the humans are doing speaks for itself. If they throw a rock or stick at us we know they're trying to hit us. We don't need to be told or understand, the same way they do, what they're doing or saying or putting on their signs. We can understand it our own way, by what we see. They never leave food or throw treats for us anymore. Not since those signs went up. You don't have to read it on a sign or have one of them tell you what they're doing. What they're doing speaks for itself and –"

"Ahh, quit saying the same thing over and over," Mel barks at him. "You're just a nervous little twit. You don't *understand* anything."

"Twitty, twitty Twitch. The nervous little –"

*** *CHAPTER 7* ***

"Shut up, Beater, or I'll –" Mel starts to threaten. Caesar makes a sharp squeak for both to be quiet.

"What the humans are doing, how they react differently to us now, speaks for itself," Twitch bravely restates, his tail jerking back and forth. He's become more agitated, because of Mel's aggressive posturing and Beater's teasing, but no less certain of his opinion.

"It seems that they've decided that fewer trees mean fewer squirrels, and that maybe no trees would mean no squirrels," Caesar explains with a tone of authority, taking over where Twitch left off.

"Who told you that?" the obviously puzzled Mel exclaims. "How the HELL could you know that?"

"It's because of what we've seen these past weeks," Caesar replies patiently. "You would have seen, too, if you were paying attention. First they were driving around in those animal control trucks and taking pictures – the white panel trucks with drawings of dogs and big nets on the doors. But they were taking pictures of us – in the trees and on the ground, wherever we happened to be – not of the people or pets. They had little books and wrote in them every time they saw one of us, like they were counting."

"Tell them about the traps, Caesar," Twitch creeps nearer to suggest. "Like the ones I –"

"Yes. They've been driving around in pairs," Caesar continues, "with a pickup truck following behind. In the bed of the pickup were stacks of those 'in but not out' kind of traps, the kind with the doors that flip down behind and catch you if you're dumb enough to go in after the bait."

"Like I used to see way out in the forest," Twitch blurts out hurriedly. "But then it was the other way around. Last winter I'd see them set one down and let whoever was inside run off. I didn't recognize any of them, though. They must have been stupid house squirrels."

"Stupid, but lucky they weren't poisoned or had their heads snapped off in a spring trap," Caesar observes, making it sound like a warning as much as information. "Anyway, yes, the traps were in the back of the pickup but they weren't setting them out. I thought that a bit strange. But I think they'll set them out soon enough. So if you see one of those long metal boxes don't go inside, no matter how good a treat seems to be in there. You'll be taken away and no telling to where." He looks around and up to make sure the others are paying attention.

"Sounds a bit far-fetched to me," Mel complains.

"Better than poison." Beryl's opinion is not much welcomed, so he adds, "People do that in their houses in the city, so I'm sure they could do that here, too."

"Well, if getting rid of us is their intention, I suppose that would be another way to do it," Caesar concedes. "But I don't think that's what they're really after. It's too sudden and too extreme. I think it's a side issue, that *we're* just a side issue. They simply want to cut down the trees, these big trees." He jerks his chin to point down at his example. "I don't know why they'd want to do that but they are. It's happening too fast. Perhaps we're being used as an excuse."

"What's your point?" Mel gruffly wants to know.

"Yes, Caesar, what's your point?" Beryl chimes in, as much to make the question stick as to minimize Mel's tenacious belligerence.

"The point is – Tell them what you told me and Sandy, Twitch," Caesar requests.

"About what I saw? What I saw in the woods?" Twitch asks, taking on an air of modest importance.

"S-s-s-sure," Sandy chatters, so as to annoy. "If it wouldn't be too much trouble."

Nervous and slightly shy, Twitch nevertheless enjoys being the center of attention. He smiles at Jolie before starting his report.

"I went pretty far into the forest, to see what's going on," he begins.

"Shouldn't have gone too far. You're so nearsighted you might not have found your way back," Beryl intrudes. "Actually, I take that back." He looks around haughtily. "We wouldn't be missing much if he didn't, actually."

"Be still, M.T.," hisses Jolie.

Beryl makes a point of seeming to ignore her but does go quiet.

"There were plenty of acorns still on the ground," Twitch continues. "So, we're good even if it's a very bad winter." His tail becoming even more active, he looks to

Caesar, who nods. "What's more important, I think," Twitch restarts, "is that people were walking from tree to tree, taking pictures and measuring how big around the trunks were. They tied these colored ribbons around some."

"To mark the ones they plan to cut down, I'll bet," Beryl again intrudes, but this time without sarcasm. "I've seen that, in the forest. They did that before the cutters came in. Then those were the trees that ended up being cut down and hauled away. Damn, now that I think of it, I saw that on a few of the big oaks way over there," he says, dropping onto all fours.

"So, what does it mean?" Jolie inquires of Caesar.

Caesar does not reply immediately but hops to the end of his branch and crouches, bobbing his head. The other squirrels peer down to where he seems to be indicating they should. None had earlier thought to take particular notice, but not far from the nearby cut stump precisely such a ribbon lies in a tangle.

Those peering down know that the smooth stump is mute evidence of the loss for many. What they cannot appreciate, of course, is that its outsized core of darker heartwood is the mute evidence of utility for some.

"What I see," Caesar then states slowly, "is that they're taking down the big oaks. Simple as that. I'm not sure I know why, exactly, but they're taking the biggest trees, the ones we build nests in, the trees that give us such tasty acorns."

*** *CHAPTER 7* ***

"These are our trees, damn it," Mel barks. "We live here."

"We may make us nests in these trees, we may forage and sleep here, even have our kits here," Beryl observes morosely in response to the interruption, "but they're not our oaks. They belong to the humans."

"Squirrels have been here as long as they have, maybe longer. What's changed?" Sandy puts to Caesar. "We want to share not take. And we make it better not worse. We even bury acorns that sprout and help replenish the oaks. Out there, anyway," he says with a nod toward Oakville's surrounding forest. "We could do that here, too, if they'd let them grow. Why be trying to get rid of us now?"

On the branches and clinging to the tree trunk, the nearby squirrels focus on Caesar. If any could answer that important question, it would be he, the oldest and the wisest. When there is only silence from him, Mel and a few others gnash their teeth – not at Caesar, certainly, but as expressions of frustrated puzzlement.

"They don't need oak saplings here. It's not a wild place like that," Caesar at last deigns to say. "They had been taking care of the big oaks pretty well. The way I see it, it's that they're trying to get rid of us but not as an end, as a means."

For everyone, even the attentive Sandy and the know-it-all Beryl, this is too subtle a point to immediately grasp.

"In other words, I think it's not us they're after. They want to take down the trees for some reason and we're the excuse. Remember those other people in big black cars stopping and looking around? That was a season ago and they didn't look at us or take pictures of us like the people in the animal control cars. They were interested in the trees. They didn't write anything down while they were watching what we did. A few smiled, is all. Then there were the people in cars driving around, the people in skin coats. They measured around the trees and looked up at how tall they were, *then* they wrote in their little books. It's the trees they were interested in and the bigger the tree, the more excited they got, the more they scribbled in their books."

"Do they want to destroy this place? Take away its trees?" Jolie asks. "Is that it?"

"They could infect the trees with a blight or bring in beetles," says Beryl. "Or spray something to kill the leaves. That would do it quicker."

"No, none of that would be quick," Sandy states. "Cutting them is quicker."

His observation suffices to set them to thinking.

"The sad part is that they have more to lose from taking down these big oaks than we do," Caesar says to them. "They're losing something that's been in Oakville for a very long time. The trees must have been very important to have grown so big. They must *never* have cut one down unless a storm or bug got to it first and it had to be. I'm sure of that."

*** *CHAPTER 7* ***

Caesar actually is making a judgment that isn't far from a guess, but he has enough good sense to realize that if these oaks are so big and the ones in the forest are so much smaller, there must be a good reason for that.

"For us," he continues, "it's not a big deal really. We'd like to stay, because these huge oaks give us lots of room and are strong shelters even in the worst storms. But, practically speaking, we can move deep into the forest. That's not going to go barren anytime soon, I don't think. But the humans? It's a bigger change for them. They're losing something they can't replace. It must take a hundred summers or more for an oak to get as big as that one was." He nods down at the stump. "Do you realize how long that is? I'm not a tenth that old. I can't conceive of being that old. But it must take at least that long, because look at how small the oak shoots still are after one or two." He runs a paw over his cheek and sniffs. "The humans must have a reason for doing what they're doing. I don't fully understand it, but I don't think it's because of us."

A general silence persists for some time. Each of the squirrels, Mae and Mel excepted perhaps, is considering what might be of help as they face the loss of their familiar habitat. To leave would be one strategy, fading into the forest and remaining there, as if Oak Park never existed. They would have to take their chances with the unfettered predators.

Resistance is another option, obviously, but equally futile to contemplate. True, the squirrels are faster and more nimble. However, the humans have much at their disposal and, more to the point, they seem to have no compunction against being cruel. A few bites, or even merely signs of aggression, and out will come the traps, perhaps even weapons and poisons that would mean the end of them.

All of this is something for the squirrels to think about.

"How about giving them a reason to stop what they're doing," Jolie therefore suggests.

"Yeah," Beater chimes in. "We can put on a charm-fest, be even cuter. We could be so cute they couldn't help but want us to stay around these oaks." He shifts about rhythmically to illustrate his point.

"Stop. You're acting like a fool," hisses Beryl.

"He *is* a fool," adds Mel.

"I think he's cute," Mae coos. "Come up and see me, Beater. Do you do more than dance?"

Mel gives her a nasty look and jumps to a higher branch.

"I think being disciplined might actually help," Beryl states. Since the essence of Beater's opinion – despite the silly antics in which it's been ensconced – seems promising, he endeavors to flesh it out. "Charging at their picnic baskets and running after the food on their plates won't make us any friends. We should stop doing things like that, so they won't be in such a hurry to destroy the places where we live."

While reasonable on its face, Beryl's suggestion seems to be too little and far too late.

"I don't see how any of that would help," Sandy says, to make that very point. He looks to Caesar for confirmation. "Not now. Not when they're already marking the trees the way they are."

"I'm afraid you're right," Caesar sighs. "It's too late for us. I don't think anything we could do would make a difference. We're an excuse not a reason."

"Then let's teach the bastards a lesson," Mel blurts out. "Gnash and chatter and bite, then. Whenever those cutters come in, run at their legs and bite them."

"If it makes you feel any better, then do that, Mel," Caesar tells him, thinking how it would probably mean it'd be his last act.

"Yeah, do it, then we'd be rid of you," Twitch says with a smirk, putting that idea into words.

"Teach them a lesson. That's your suggestion, is it, Mel?" Beryl lifts himself up and shakes his head then his body. "They're not going to understand us any more than we understand them. It'd give them more reason to get rid of us and only make things worse."

"Things seem very bad now," Jolie says. "How can they get any worse?"

Caesar turns in her direction.

"Bad can always get worse," he tells her.

"And the other problem with teaching a lesson is," Sandy elaborates, "that what's learned isn't always what you wanted to teach."

"Very wise, Sandy." Caesar's compliment is sincere. "I'm glad to see that. This might be my last winter. Remember, when you take over, that it isn't us they're after. It's like, we're being made out to be a problem that needs to be dealt with and taking down the oaks is the way to do that. But I believe it's exactly the opposite: Taking down the oaks is what they're after and making us undesirable is the way to make *that* seem necessary, the right thing to do." Caesar nods vigorously. "It's obvious that the large oaks have been part of their city for many, many years. I can't imagine what could be their real reason for cutting them down now. But you can be sure it isn't because of us. It's despite us." He passes a heavy sigh. "They'll regret it. The bad that humans do lives after them. These changes," he slowly turns his head to scan the nearby trees, "won't make things better for them. It'll make them worse. And they're not going to realize that until after we and the big oaks are gone. Then it'll be too late."

CHAPTER EIGHT

Nathan chose a different topic for his term paper and received a good grade. He was pleased.

With the new growth that came with spring, Oak Park was dramatically different. The many huge, pale stumps with dark centers made the grassy vistas seem more expansive. There were more bushes but fewer birds, because there was left only a marginal scattering of high tree branches for them to perch upon. As often happens when an ecological void is created, much less welcome creatures took their place – the pigeons. Useless creatures that provide scant entertainment and much mess, they were for another city administration to deal with. But first, of course, there would need to appear a rationale. Also, some would have to benefit concretely from doing so.

*** *CHAPTER 8* ***

*   *   *   *   *

Spring passed, its end ushering in meteorological summer with its high sun. Fewer families came to spread out blankets for picnics, play with their children, or walk their dogs. The prior mild and cloudy few months had been more suitable for such small pleasures, because the only way to have shade was to bring it, in the form of rickety canopies or beach umbrellas, which few had or intended to purchase. Playing hide-and-seek was less of a game because of the absence of thick-bodied trees. The impressions that Oak Park went on forever and would be forever, that it was for busy arboreal creatures as well as for humans trying to relax, were compromised by the recently completed steel fencing that marked the border between it and the native forest beyond. This was mandated by consistency, the need to reinforce the impression that the squirrels of the forest must be kept out.

Set deep into the ground and of smooth metal, the fence could not be burrowed under nor climbed, even by creatures whose habit it is to burrow or have sharp claws with which to cling. Its narrow slits were impossible for any squirrel to squeeze though. Uninterrupted by any usable opening, even one gated and locked, a ball or balloon or wind-blown hat was forever lost if it crossed over. While incidental and unrelated to the stated main purpose of the fencing, this changed expectations. Industrially secure, the fencing was fundamentally paradoxical. Proclaimed to be unobtrusive, it focused attention on that which wasn't meant to be seen. Fortunately the baited traps and poisoned nut cakes, which were set out during late winter and for much of the spring, had done their job and were gone.

There remained only a paltry representation of the massive, ancient oaks still standing when the last meeting of the Oakville City Council before the summer break was called to order. Councilman Epps presented a "suggestion" from one of his constituents to the effect that, in view of the changes, Oak Park needed to be renamed. Supported at length by Dwight Eisen and quickly seconded, the topic was flagged to be a key item when city business was again taken up in the fall.

Perhaps a poll should be conducted in the interim, the dapper and accommodating Dwight Eisen additionally had suggested.

Hays Bales swiped across the back of his broad neck with the handkerchief he had been holding throughout the entirety of this council session.

"Could we just do that informally, Mister Eisen? Everyone is looking forward to a wonderful, wonderful summer and no extra responsibilities."

"Of course, Mister Mayor," Eisen responded. "I'll casually ask around for suggestions."

The park was still being used by Oakville's citizens but not as before. No one came to compose photographs or sketch. Wedding and betrothal assemblies necessarily took place elsewhere. Special anniversaries and birthdays were celebrated in backyards or commercial facilities. Few came to the soon to be renamed Oak Park to eat their lunch during the middle of a busy day. The occasional dog playing fetch with its master or lone skater speeding on one of its paved paths had few to contend with. It was rare to see older citizens, who traditionally have few external constraints, making use of it. Its uncovered benches were too stressful in the sun. The newly abundant clear space had made kite flying popular during the blustery spring. In the doldrums of summer, that activity, also, waned.

* * * * *

On this morning of a relatively cool, early September day, a visibly tired Mayor Bales and his aide, Brevan Shannon, have situated themselves on a bench that faces the slope down toward where one of the biggest oaks once stood. Their view is unencumbered. Some would describe it as without character, even insipid.

"The first council meeting's coming up soon isn't it?"

Brevan scans the increased bulk of his boss and brushes some crumbs, from the muffin just consumed, off his own wrinkled slacks.

"Shouldn't have had that," he observes. "I gained quite a bit over the summer.... That's right. It's next Wednesday." He lets loose a heavy sigh as he rubs a finger back and forth under his nose. "Time's going by awfully fast, it seems. In a few weeks I'll stand next to some young buck, put my hand on his shoulder, tell the crowd 'Here is your new Councilman!' and start planning the campaign. Maybe I'll push a woman to run."

"You think you'd be able to say 'Councilwoman' without stuttering over it?"

"I'll practice," Shannon laughs.

"Well, you're right about the time slipping away. I think I've had enough of city work, Brevan. It's become tedious, very tedious. Maya wants to take another cruise or two.... I've got enough put away now," Bales says between thoughtful nods.

"All you'll do is sit, stare, and eat."

Bales studies his paunch.

"I don't think that'd be so bad," he says. "Not so bad. Sitting quiet seems a very good plan, a very good plan."

"That makes you sound old, Hays."

Bales forms his lips into a slight pucker. "I think you're right," he says. "It does. Old and tired. Haven't you had enough of the hoorah and the be-my-buddy smiles?"

"If you're not going to run," Shannon says without answering directly, "then maybe I should. Make it my final goodbye."

"Be serious, Brevan. That's not your thing. You're a behind the scenes sort. As mayor you'd spend most of your time on stage and get paid practically nothing. The easy pickings are gone. We rode it at the right time." Bales pauses and puts on a pained, thoughtful expression. "Let the college-smart gentlemen with lots of high class social ideas fight over it. Like that Steinberg or Feinberg guy, whatever. Eisen's buddy. Their kind love showing off how much they know and claiming they're going to make the world a better place."

"Right," Shannon laughs. "Let them try. They deserve it."

The way in which he delivers his opinion makes it more insult than suggestion.

Footsteps behind cause both to turn their heads

"If you wore softer shoes, Marcus, we never would've heard you," Bales tells Epps.

"I wasn't trying to sneak," the latter protests. "Sylvia told me.... She said this is where you probably went off to. Hello, Brevan."

Shannon nods back. He and Bales shift to one side to make room for the new arrival.

"Looking for me? Or just out for a healthy walk?" the latter unnecessarily asks.

"Well, for you, mainly. But both really. I'm antsy.... It's been a rotten summer." Epps puffs out his cheeks. "We never went anywhere this year, except to visit her sick mother for a couple weeks."

Bales knows the man is referring to his mother-in-law on the Maine coast. He prefers, however, not to receive more diagnostic or prognostic details than he'd already been treated to before the summer began.

"I've never been. What's it like up there during July and August?" Bales segues. "It should've been much, much cooler, at least."

"The mosquitoes made pretty good meals of me, I'll say that. Couldn't do much but stay around the house.... She has AC and doesn't like to go out.... I don't like to fish."

Shannon crosses his legs and looks into the bland distance, waiting to hear the reason for Epps having sought them out. Sensing the same, Bales leans his head back slightly as if searching upwards. He squints and watches the sun start to peek out from behind a cloud.

"I'm worried," Epps finally admits.

"What are you worried about, Marcus?" Bales inquires politely. "Have people come tapping on your office door already? Campaign donors home from their trips and anxious for their payback, maybe?"

"Not that exactly. Several have come in to complain about what's happened to this park."

"Serious or just whiners?" Bales wants to ascertain, although he could not articulate what he would extract from any such distinction.

"A little of both, I think."

"Tell them not to worry," Shannon contributes. His views are constant and firm. "In the long run they won't notice the difference. They'll forget about it."

"The long run, yes," Epps sighs. "But I don't want them pestering me in the short run."

"Good point," Bales replies. "I've been thinking along the very same lines. As I was saying to Brevan here, come November I'll be happy to see someone else take over. Maybe it should be you. What do you think?"

Epps doesn't immediately react. He leans over his knees instead, to study the ground.

"Seriously. Why not run for mayor?" Bales suggests explicitly. "I'll stand up for you." He looks to one side. "And I've got a very, very good person here to suggest for making sure it's a successful campaign."

Brevan is careful not to say or do anything.

"I hadn't considered that, Hays." Epps glances at Shannon before focusing on Mayor Bales. "But, I was thinking.... What if I got out of politics, took a position with Putter Hardwoods instead? He has projects downstate similar to ours here and has made me an offer," he goes on to say.

"That'd be the thing to do if you don't like having people knocking on your door with an agenda," Bales informs him. "But they'd be knocking on your door with a task sheet. And telling, not asking."

"Sure. You'd have to work for a living," Shannon adds semi-seriously, "and give up playing at real estate."

"Exactly, exactly," Mayor Bales seconds. "It might not be as pleasant as Putter makes it seem. The money may not be worth it. But, seriously, being a mayor? I'd think about that carefully, very carefully, if I were you. You'd have to deal with a steady stream of people coming to your office. With any luck, some with more than an agenda in their hands," he laughs. "But you do that anyway. I know, buck stopper isn't what you're used to. But it's easy if you have a thick skin and get the right staff to do the work. The hardest part is getting elected." He smiles toward Brevan Shannon. "All downhill after that." He chooses to deflect Epps' concerns rather than address them directly. The man has always been too much of a thinker for him, someone to use but at a distance. "And many fine, very fine opportunities will come along. Real estate and politics are a good match, especially in a tight little city like this."

"Well ..." Marcus sighs, briefly visualizing the potentialities. He's not an overly greedy person and, if energized by circumstance, might make a good chief executive for Oakville. "I'm not sure I'd enjoy being the one in charge. Too much pressure.... Actually, I like what I do right now. For the most part, anyway. It's just that I'm getting some blowback, some resentment about the loss of the big trees," he says to return to his prior mild complaint. "Is there something we should do about that?"

"The park hasn't been lost," Brevan partially restates so as to contradict. "Not lost at all, Look." He points downslope. "We, they, have just taken down some trees. It's been made better, in fact," he casts smiles upon the gentlemen to either side.

"Taken big trees," Epps sighs. "The biggest and the oldest, yes.... A few have complained that they were what made Oakville different, what made it attractive."

"You're making a big deal out of a few malcontents," Shannon scoffs. "The trees are gone to Putter's mill. That discussion is over. There'll always be complainers. No matter what you do, there's always someone out there who's going to crab about it."

"He's right, you know," Mayor Bales adds. "Do what you think is best, what gets you the most, and get on with it."

"What's best for the city, you mean."

"Certainly, Marcus. Certainly, certainly. What's best for the city. What gets the most for the city," Bales effuses.

"I still don't know what I should do," Epps complains.

"What do you want to do?" Brevan quite reasonably asks.

"The city's business, I suppose. Only, I think it's more that I've been at it so long I don't know what else I *would* do. Serving on the council doesn't pay that much, directly, but I have plenty of free time and it really is good for my real estate business ... and other things."

"Tell you what, Marcus. What about this?" Mayor Bales puts to his long time colleague. "Stay put but work on giving them and whoever takes charge something else to worry about besides the damn trees. Put together some penny projects that they can do something about. Something for the voters," he grins, "smiley-face crap that'll keep their minds off the important, dollar deals they shouldn't be worrying about." He grins and winks at his ever useful but disheveled aide. "Shannon, here, will think of something for you."

The three stare, past the still bright new fence, at the forest beyond. They don't attempt to pierce its mysteries. Their concerns are focused on themselves, "like it should be," as Bales would no doubt say. That the park has changed doesn't concern them. That the squirrels are gone doesn't concern them. That some, as Epps has reported, are troubled by both of these doesn't concern them. Their pecuniary focus had made their lives comfortable. They trust that it will continue to be so. But, and this is key, at their age and at their station it really doesn't make much difference. Their primary concerns have been for themselves and they have far more past than future.

*   *   *   *   *

It doesn't take going deep into the woods to find new young oaks having taken root. There are no hundred year old examples, but there's sufficient growth to still have the area be called a forest. Some would claim that the Founders Oaks represented an experiment, a local application of what people from The Old Country sensed should be and could be. What had been attempted in Oakville met with several centuries of success, it must be acknowledged. Perhaps, however, experiments provide as much insight by their failures as by their successes. Something new always evolves from each.

Acorns, the seeds of the oaks, their future, are abundant in Oakville's surrounding forest and the ground is fertile, ready for the proper time and the proper configuration of sun and rain. No longer in Oak Park, the squirrels yet are not so distant. They are simply elsewhere, doing what they did, making their way through the seasons. Some have died and young kits have appeared. Their identity endures, only their locale has changed.

On and beneath the branches of a stand of mid-sized oaks deep into Oakville's surrounding forest, several squirrels have paused their customary pursuits to gather close.

"He just never woke up," Sandy is in the midst of explaining.

"You could say the same when he was alive," Mel scoffs.

"That's mean to say, Mel," Mae chides him. "Caesar meant well, even if he couldn't do well."

"Anyway, he was old. I'm surprised Caesar lived as long as he did," M.T. muses. He sits upright on the branch, at the trunk end where it's stable in the slight breeze, and strikes an uncharacteristically pensive pose. "All the seasons he talked about sounded crazy. Just like it was weird to hear him talk about my parents. I don't even remember them."

**** CHAPTER 8 ****

Mel wrinkles his nose and moves farther from Beryl. "One mother and a dozen fathers. Of course you don't remember them."

Mel sniffs and scowls, but M.T. Beryl, who has grown both wiser by example from Sandy and more tolerant by virtue of age, does not react. Sandy gives him a look of approval. He's about to say something but is interrupted by a figure landing amongst the leaves at the end of his branch.

"Chitter chatter, chitter chatter. That's all y'do's chitter chatter," Beater syncopates in his cloying, singsong manner. "Chitter chatter bop-bop-hop. Chitter chatter hop." His more mature look makes this, as well as his other antics, less sincere and certainly less entertaining. Beater becomes suddenly self-conscious and still, a most unusual mien for him.

Beryl gives him a look of disdain. Perhaps, he thinks, if Beater would nest with an accepting female, he'd finally mature and accept his true nature.

As if he has insight into Beryl's thoughts, Sandy shakes his head.

"Are you ever going to grow up, Beater? Or is hopping about all you're capable of?"

"I can do more," counters Beater, refusing to be contrite. "But why? What I do is more fun."

"Hopeless," Sandy says, almost to himself. Then to Beryl and the others nearby he calls out, "What's with the acorn crop? Is everyone at it?"

A ragged chorus of affirmation comes from nearby branches, with most of the responders being unseen.

"Looking good, yes," Beryl responds directly. "We'll be fine this winter." Then, gazing disapprovingly at Beater who, like Mel, he knows does less than his share, he adds, "Most of us."

"What about on the other side of the fence?" Beater asks, sounding almost normal.

"Who th'hell goes there anymore?" Mel responds crabbily and rhetorically. "There are no trees, so there aren't going to be any damn nuts."

"I liked the treat treats the humans would leave leave," Beater confesses, reverting to his characteristic syncopation.

"Talk normal, Beater, would you please? You showed that you could.... Anyway, those were bad for us," Sandy states, looking away. "I don't know why humans find them so irresistible. Acorns are much tastier. And better for you, I'd have to say. It's just as well that we don't go there."

"Right," Mel agrees. "The nuts here are plenty big."

"Ohhh, they certainly are, Big Boy," Mae coos suggestively to her paramour. "And so's what comes with them."

Mel is sated and pays her no mind. Finding her tiresome and hackneyed after these many months, he's less inclined to be seen with her during daylight. Seeming to detect this, the change in Mel's manner that has being developing since late spring, she turns and disappears to the opposite side of the trunk, soon to be seen several branches above, next to an obviously immature squirrel. He is one of this year's and begins to vigorously rub his forepaws against his chest.

"There are so many," Beryl continues, "that they're washing down into the creek before we can get to them. Even the deer have more than enough."

"Probably another cold, cold winter is coming, then," Sandy observes. "That's what Caesar used to say when ... Anyway, good. It makes sense to take advantage of a bigger crop when we have one. Can't hurt. What we don't eat will sprout and, with the lumbermen so busy here lately, the forest can use that."

"You and M.T. have become quite the pair," says Jolie to Sandy. Her sudden appearance startles him. He hadn't noticed her scrambling up the trunk. "You know a lot and he knows the rest, so between you, you know everything."

"I wish you wouldn't still be calling me that," Beryl complains.

Jolie's tone is light, as if she really doesn't mean to be insulting. There is, however, a somber note in her voice. Something is troubling her.

"Have you seen Twitch recently?" she asks. "I've been looking everywhere for him."

"I saw him by the creek; creep creepin' by the creek creek," Beater lilts, being only marginally helpful.

"No. Haven't seen him," Beryl contributes, gnashing his incisors at the once again childlike Beater. "He's gone exploring, I'll wager."

"Have you checked up top?" Sandy asks with a head motion toward the thinning canopy.

"Yes, earlier," Jolie replies.

All are silent.

A long distance away, near the creek that is much shallower and more slow moving now that the season is changing, a bright metal box, with its sides of wire mesh of the type called hardware cloth, sits at the base of a tree. Inside the box, a rigid, spring loaded metal bar has pinned a squirrel by its neck. It must have come down very hard because trickles of blood have oozed from the squirrel's mouth and nose, staining what remains of the tempting nut cake on the floor of the box. Neither human nor squirrel was close enough to hear the bar snap down, however. And now there is only silence. The creature's once hyperactive tail gives one more twitch then becomes still, as still as its bulging eyes, as still as the few stubborn oak leaves on the branches above.

*   *   *   *   *

Putter's company got what it wanted, the furniture makers got what they wanted, and Mayor Bales and those allied with him got what they wanted. It didn't much matter what the residents of Oakville wanted. They were too well managed to organize a constituency that had to be reckoned with. In fact, they were treated to such a surfeit of rationale that they came to feel that they, also, got what they wanted. Or, at least, they were sufficiently mollified not to clamor that they hadn't.

Respected social scientists and satirists have written that it's good when people become fed up with angry politics, that, when they finally have had enough of divisiveness, they will turn away from it and focus on their own lives. This, they claim, is what energizes democracy, what makes it more robust. Nothing is further from the truth. To look upon that escapism as a good sign could not be more ominous for democracy. Nothing is more desired by those who would mislead and control than such an eventuality. **Lethargic, yet assiduously sculpted acceptance makes political manipulation feasible.** This is the social realism that should be de rigueur for their treatises and tomes.

The ancient oaks of Oak Park were deemed a liability because of the squirrels. If the latter had posed a serious problem, then the poisons and traps were certainly justifiable. But the argument in their disfavor flowed in the opposite direction. The orchestrated necessity for their depletion was a means to a quite different end. It became a sufficient reason for the removal of their urban habitat, their preferred home, and for putting it, that collection of stately, old trees, to better use.

Then why that added insult of traps and poisons? The squirrels never presented an existential threat to Oakville or its citizenry. Political expediency required, however, that once having been labeled undesirable, a danger, the squirrels had to be treated as such. They had to be painted as reprehensible and incorrigible. Their displacement had to be elevated to the point of being unavoidable, an "at any cost" solution. Thus framed, the mandate desired by Mayor Bales could take the form of unimpeded action. How prosaic this seems in retrospect. Yet, it seems that the squirrels were more prone to recognize the deception than the humans.

The huge oaks of Oak Park are gone. Even if some reversal were to be contemplated, it would occur far in the future. The benefits were short lived and unique to a few. The consequences, on the other hand, will last for decades and will affect many.

Much the same is happening in the natural forests surrounding Oakville. While this will likewise progress, the citizens of Oakville show little inclination to attend to that which, the majority argues, is not their concern. But that will prove to be seriously wrong. It's an expression of uninterest not disinterest. Trends and changes in perception have their own momentum. The consequences of unwise acts flow forward regardless of whether or not the full spectrum of results exceeds actual intent. What is happening around Oakville will make any reversal of what has already happened there that much more distant. Sturdy, towering oaks may never reemerge. The simple fact is that their Founders Oaks lacked an effective coterie of champions. The ephemera of nostalgia, the aura of familiarity, and the meager recognition of their significance were impotent for that purpose. So quickly taken down, there is only the memory of those stately trees. And that, also, is easy to manipulate.

CHAPTER NINE

Nearly thirty years after the last ancient oak was taken from their park, the biggest issue before the citizens of Oakville is titular: Is it time to change the city's name? Some have suggested that the reference has become tenuous. Others offer more forward-looking reasons. The city should chart a new future, for example, and its name should reflect that. Those in charge haven't yet decided what this new name could or should be, what would best suit their interests and, "of course, of course," the interests of the citizens. They are, therefore, unable to plan the political tactics that would ensure the renaming receives popular support.

Their park provides much the same pleasures as before. Office workers are there during lunch breaks. Runners and walkers appear during the earlier and later parts of the day. Any sort of wheeled contrivance is still banned from the paved paths, of which there are many more, now that there is so much more open space. Concrete tables with matching benches are set out in no particular arrangement. A few are under cover in recognition of the fact that there is no leafy protection. They and the scattered metal benches, also provided for visitors' use, are numbered, as if their locations on some map were of significance.

Shallow depressions and soft hills of green comprise the vast majority of the park. The native grass has been nearly totally replaced by synthetic, courtesy of another lucrative contract that benefitted, like the paving, several on the City Council. There were ample justifications, of course: It was safer; maintenance costs were significantly reduced; unwanted pests were precluded. Picnickers are rarely seen, even on mild summer days, however. It's hard to substitute the smell and feel of plastic and base material for that of fertile soil and freshly cut turf.

At the rough edge of the park, where few go now, darkly stained stumps can still be seen. Low to the ground, rimmed by pale ears of fungi, and framed by the scour of erosion, they are evidence of less than diligent grinding decades ago when the mutilations were fresh. Time, weather, and the natural processes of decay henceforth had to suffice.

This being a pleasant Sunday, Nathan has suggested a brief outing, something his boys should enjoy in contrast to the confinement of an apartment and their complex's geometric, cookie-cutter environs. He, more so than many, has a history of visiting the park with family and feels the need to renew that. His wife, Jennifer, and he are striving for the day when they can afford a single family house with even a minimal patch of grass – real grass – at the back.

This late morning Nathan pulls the time stamped parking pass from the machine and places it on the dashboard of their hybrid as the twins help their mother with the blanket and a few lightweight lawn chairs. The lidded picnic case will be his responsibility. His is one of the few private vehicles in evidence. He's able to park it at the edge of the blacktop, adjacent to the edge of the "grass" and well away from the corporate fun-food shops that have come to occupy large sections of the park.

"Tommy, Timmy, set those over there, at the top of the slope," he calls out to the boys. "Fetch these after that."

He throws out a metal bat, two gloves, and a scuffed softball in their general direction.

The boys will not mind sitting on the blanket spread out over the fake grass, which is more for looking than for sitting. Their parents prefer chairs. Nathan moves his closer to his wife's and sits. Both can remember the smell and feel of natural growth. He stretches out his legs and releases a lengthy sigh.

"Busy week. And next week'll be even busier."

"Don't talk about work, Sweetheart," his wife replies. "Just relax. You've been so tense lately."

*** *CHAPTER 9* ***

"Have to hit our marks, Jen. Have to hit our marks. Those who don't, get docked. They're always watching."

"Well, forget about that, at least for today."

"I used to come here a lot with my mom and dad, when I was the twins' age," he relates once he's relented. "We'd sit on the grass right over ..." He looks about, trying to spot an identifying landmark but cannot. He signifies an unspoken thought by lifting both hands then letting them drop heavily onto his lap.

"What did you do?" she asks.

"Not much. It was just nice to get somewhere where it was cool and fresh outside. Mom would make sandwiches, and we'd watch birds and the squirrels."

"Squirrels? I've never seen a squirrel here. That must have been way before I moved here."

"It was. I grew up here. There were huge oaks trees and ... Well, anyway, I remember it was fun to watch them scurry around the park and to throw them leftover bits from our picnics. Especially in the fall, when they were active."

He stands up and calls out to the twins: "Let's hit a few, before snack time. Okay?"

The twins had wandered off only a short distance and run back when summoned, with Tommy in the lead and Timmy trying to pass him. The softball Nathan has brought is very soft indeed. He doesn't have to worry about it carrying very far when he, nor certainly they, hit it. After several alternations of who is batter, pitcher, or fielder, Nathan flips the glove onto the small blanket.

"Let's have those sandwiches. That sound good?"

Having rushed through their breakfast, the two boys respond in an enthusiastic chorus. Timmy's enthusiasm exceeds his judgment and the ball that he attempts to pitch onto the blanket misses the mark. It rolls down the slope toward the tall, discolored metal fence that still separates the park from the woods, that old growth of trees most refer to simply as "the forest."

"You go get it, smart guy," Nathan smiles at the lad. He watches as his son retrieves the ball then reaches into the overgrown real grass that has managed to survive at the base of the fence. Timmy picks something up. Their softball in one hand, he turns and holds up what appears to be a rectangle affixed to a length of metal or wood.

"Bring it here," Nathan calls out.

Once Timmy is close to their blanket, Nathan is sorry that he made that request.

"Careful! That's old metal and looks rusty. The broken end of the post may be sharp," he tells the boy.

Timmy holds the sign away from his body and turns it toward his father. He drops the ball onto the blanket.

"What does it mean?" he asks. "I know the red circle with a bar across it means 'Don't!' but what's that animal?"

"That's a squirrel, Timmy. It's an old 'Don't feed the squirrels' sign," Nathan explains. "They decided to get rid of them, to keep them out of the park and away from the big trees that used to be here. Someone must have thrown the sign down by the fence. Set it over there. And be careful!"

Timmy does as told. Both of the boys then look toward the fence.

"If there weren't squirrels here, then why would they have to tell you not to feed them?" Timmy quite rationally asks.

"I know why there's a fence," Tommy volunteers. "It's so you don't go over there. It's not safe, Teacher said."

"Everyone knows *that*," Timmy says, so as not to be left behind. He's still waiting for an answer to his question.

"No, the woods aren't safe, I imagine," Jennifer states. "Only lumbermen and hunters go there."

"In a way, I guess that's true," Nathan says. "But I remember when they put that fence up. I was still in school. Before then, my buddies and I had used to go there a lot. The fence was needed to keep the squirrels out, the city said."

"They must really not've liked them," Tommy observes. "That's a really big old fence."

"No," Nathan laughs, "they didn't. They decided the squirrels shouldn't be so friendly with the people." He points to the discarded sign. "They told everyone to stop giving them little treats, like bits of leftover cookies or sandwich crusts from their picnics. We used to like to do that when I was your age." He smiles. "Your Aunt Vicky and I. But then they decided the squirrels had to go. Told us they were dangerous and that we shouldn't feed them. Pretty soon they chased them out. They cut down the big oak trees and stuck that fence up so they wouldn't come back."

"What big trees?" Timmy wonders aloud, having been distracted from his original query. "I don't see any trees in the park now."

"Of course not, stupid," Tommy says with a knowledgeable frown. "There never were any."

"But Daddy just said they cut them down," Timmy protests. He looks to his father. "Didn't you just say they cut down big trees?"

"They did, Timmy," Nathan says.

"No, they didn't," Tommy insists. "Teacher told us about the park and showed us old pictures. There were never any big trees here. She had us write a report about the park and I used my tablet to look up all about it. You did, too," he throws at his brother, who pouts and glowers back. "Don't you ever remember anything?"

"Stop, boys. I'll just tell you that there were, because I used to come here when I was your age and run around them. My daddy, your grandpa, told me the story of how they got to be here, how the people that started Oakville a long, long time ago planted them. Some got so big around that I could stand behind and your Auntie Vicky couldn't even see me."

Nathan again smiles, this time at the mental picture of his little sister chasing him around a thick, rough trunk and of his being just fast enough so she couldn't catch him.

"I'm going to get my tablet and prove it to you," Tommy tells Timmy in a firm tone. He's certain of the veracity of his instruction and readings.

"Go ahead." Nathan motions to the car and unlocks it with his fob. "I want to see that, too," he adds more loudly, raising his eyebrows to his wife as Timmy chases after his brother. He's confident that, when accessed properly, the boys' tablets will confirm his recollections. How could they not? "Don't bring both," he thinks to calls out. "You just need one."

When the two boys return, Tommy turns on his tablet. He peers at its screen, waiting.

"Pleaze, pleaze! A Choco-freeze!" emanates from the thin device.

Nathan grimaces.

"Does it always do that?" he asks Jennifer.

"Whenever they turn it on." She shakes her head. "And whenever they get enough points on one of their games. Drives me crazy sometimes, because it's always so loud."

"Pleaze, pleaze! A Choco-freeze!" the tablet repeats.

"Do a Go-Search, Tommy," Nathan tells him curtly. He has heard quite enough of what the tablet wants to say. "Try Oakville Founders Oaks," he advises and waits.

"Pleaze, pleaze! A Choco-freeze!"

"Mute it, Tommy!" Nathan demands. "I don't want to keep hearing that.... What does it show?"

"Nothing about big old trees."

"Try Oakville, history."

Nathan waits patiently, watching Tommy scan the silenced screen. Tommy shakes his head.

"Nothing about a park with big trees, Dad. It just says what I wrote in my report, that," he peers down, "'Oakville has kept its old park in its natural state.'"

"Let me see. Fake grass isn't much of a natural state," Nathan scoffs. He takes the tablet from Tommy and attempts the search several different ways. He, too, reads from the screen, patiently – at least at first – scrolling through page after page. He finds nothing to contradict his son's assertion or to confirm his.

"See," Tommy says boldly. "You were wrong. The park was always like this. There were never any big trees here. The pictures show it just like this."

"Well, I remember them," his father repeats softly.

"Teacher says you can't trust what people say they remember. People forget or get mixed up. It's what's on Go-Search that's true. That doesn't get mixed up. People forget things too easy, she said."

Nathan has no immediate way to verify that his recollection is correct, to establish the prior existence of the once proud Founders Oaks and the facts of their history or of the squirrels that frequented them. Certainly, he could take the twins for a walk to the far edge of the park and show them the remains of a stump or two, but that would not resonate with them. It would not compel them to believe the vision of the past he's trying to impart. Some old pictures might be of help, some palpable documentary evidence. He sighs in mild frustration and thinks of the book tucked away in his desk drawer, the desk that was his late father's. He had inherited both but, for some reason, it was the former that carried the most meaning. It was the former he had felt more attached to and vowed would be the more meaningful memento to pass on to his sons. Now he believes he knows why he had harbored that compulsion and is glad he did.

"Too easily, you should say, Tommy," Nathan belatedly corrects. "But, yes, that seems to be exactly right. It is far too easy to forget."

His mind is divided. He hears what his son is saying and is reluctant to cause him conflict by contradicting what the young boy has been taught in school and by his tablet. Yet, he knows that isn't true. He has the images from his own memory and they are firm. And he has more. He has what his father told him and the book that verifies it, that reifies it. Perhaps it's time to sit the boys down and talk about that, time for them to know what time and circumstance have really brought about, not just what their instructors and their damn tablets want them to know. Nathan nods slowly as he muses. Yes, he thinks, show them the pictures and tell them what happened.

*** *CHAPTER 9* ***

He leans slightly forward, one hand massaging the other. But why? he asks himself silently. Is there any point when they're this young? They'll just judge his faithfully retained text to be a fake and his memory flawed, as how most of what is contrary to the current desired ethic is framed. Yes, they'll complain that it's a book full of false facts and that he's trying to fool them. What they're told in class, what they read and hear from their tablets, these form the foundation of their reality.

"Have a question? Use Go-Search," all are now encouraged. Rely on that singular portal, which enables uniformity and directed opinion to make the private and personal mesh perfectly with the mercantile/social matrix. By design, instilled habit and constant circulation of the common lore will be hard to overcome. It's the peer pressure of wearing the torn jeans and logoed pullovers of his youth transformed into the acceptance of disembodied authority, an authority that derives its power from, paradoxically, seeming to be distributed while in fact being singular. The tools once used to sell products have been honed for the selling of ideas, for molding history and thereby the future.

Nathan knows he can offer nothing to compete with any of it, not until Tommy and Timmy are older and better able to think for themselves. He has two profound hopes. Firstly, that such a day will dawn and, secondly, that it won't be far off. Surely they'll come to be reminded of what has been lost or to conceive anew what could be found. His counterbalancing fear is that his hopes won't be realized. He can't formalize it but knows instinctively that ingrained beliefs start small but grow large, like the massive oaks that spring from diminutive acorns. They last for generations until cut down and replaced by new norms.

*   *   *   *   *

Surprisingly, few would claim that Oakville has regressed in the three decades since Mayor Bales' tenure. This, also, is by design. Nothing lasts forever, even loss. New oaks have taken root in the forest surrounding it. That restoration may have happened without the aid of squirrels but certainly some, more diligent than others in burying acorns where they would flourish, can take partial credit. New oaks have arisen there despite the conscious efforts – whether arising from practical, mercantile, or philosophical considerations, or simply from ignorance and spite – to cut them down.

In Oakville itself, the stately oaks that dated from the city's founding remain only as a memory, for some, and as historical notations hidden away in sequestered printed texts for others. Probing and analysis are discouraged. Each has been diminished, both directly by misrepresentation and indirectly by guided encouragement of other pursuits. It's better that way. Focusing on the past and what it could teach is too heavy a burden upon the present. Too burdensome, at least, for those who have evolved to manage it.

Oak Park was renamed but not after Hays Bales, as he had fervently sought. His passing, a few years after leaving office, was noted but neither celebrated nor lamented. He was too small a figure to have earned a great measure of either. Momentary notoriety was what he earned and what he gained. He left a legacy, without doubt, but not one a person, such as Nathan, with unsullied memories, would adjudge favorable.

People still work and raise their families in Oakville. But life is different from that of a generation ago. That few notice the changes and lament them is testimony to the effectiveness of incidental training conditioned by invoked necessity. Some, in fact, have found life more manageable without constant reminders of their history. The consequent release from implied obligations is welcome.

History may delimit an era's end or beginning, depending on point of view, but for those living on the cusp of the change, only the small, incidental variations are perceived. The practical concerns that dominate daily lives are at the fore. Making each day pleasant and ushering in the next consumes the vast part of their attention. With a large fraction each life conditioned by the guardians of a hyperconnected world, the most important becomes the most managed, by which there is then little need for thoughtful consideration. Social stability of that sort can persist for a long time, right up until the upward pressure of rights has been unwisely allowed to grow so strong as to challenge the downward pressure of privilege. The small voices, the hidden thoughts then are amplified and receive notice. The discontented few find fertile ground, upon which a new forest of ideals can spring up.

Like trees, common knowledge grows large from small beginnings. New ideas, carefully crafted and cast upon well-prepared ground, can achieve remarkable acceptance. Lacking absolutes, it remains, as always, for history to be the judge of which are to be celebrated versus mourned.

THE END